John Buchan

Sir Walter Ralegh

The Stanhope essay, 1897

John Buchan

Sir Walter Ralegh
The Stanhope essay, 1897

ISBN/EAN: 9783337394073

Printed in Europe, USA, Canada, Australia, Japan

Cover: Foto ©Andreas Hilbeck / pixelio.de

More available books at **www.hansebooks.com**

SIR WALTER RALEGH

THE STANHOPE ESSAY, 1897

BY

JOHN BUCHAN

EXHIBITIONER OF BRASENOSE COLLEGE

Oxford

B. H. BLACKWELL, 50 AND 51 BROAD STREET

LONDON: SIMPKIN, MARSHALL, HAMILTON, KENT & CO.

1897

SIR WALTER RALEGH

I.

THERE are certain characters apparent on the page of history which at a first glance seem to be treated with scant justice or with an extravagant kindliness. We find them dismissed with a curt note, assigned to a very little niche in the house of fame, and branded as insignificant: in which case we are left to wonder at the extraordinary and dispro-portioned vitality of such reputations in the popular mind. Or, again, it may happen that out of deference to fame they are treated at immoderate length, till we feel the compara-tive smallness of their actual achievement, when added to the lengthy narration of their lives, to be something in the nature of an anti-climax.

The endowment of popularity, whether or not it be allied with true and lasting greatness, is always a difficult, elusive quality to estimate. Some have it in the highest degree; others not at all: and in any case mere popular favour is not in itself a thing of paramount importance. Influence upon national institutions, upon the mechanism of legal and political administration, upon public life and character—these are the proper gifts with which history credits the great ; and it is clear that none of these, save the last, has any necessary connexion with the kindly notoriety given by tradition and story. Hence, in the case of those elect spirits whose gifts or fate have had something of that dazzling romantic quality which leads captive a people's heart, it must be the part of history to use especial discrimination.   It is the historian's duty to explain such fame by the attributes of the man, but further to enumerate dispassionately his achievements and form some estimate of character apart from the gaudy popular portrait.   And the task is a hard one, for often the honest inquirer is compelled to trample upon cherished ideals and do violence to honest sentiment, since the prevailing power of truth is not so confidently admitted as her greatness.   He is happy who can use critical research only to brighten the colours and make the lines more brilliant, and at the end find his task to have been the justification and not the challenging of the people's verdict.

The case of Sir Walter Ralegh has been somewhat after this order. ⌣His fate it has been to live as a memory in English hearts, to have his name used as a synonym for high-hearted valour, and to shine resplendent in many monographs; while in serious history he has either usurped a major place by virtue of his reputation, or suffered the neglect of one who has left few tangible results.   His many biographers have almost invariably fallen into the fatal trick of eulogy, and the ordinary reader is still perplexed with a gallery of contradictory portraits. ⸝ The fair scholarly history of his life and deeds is yet to be written—a history which should attempt to build up from the multitudinous records of the time the vigorous, complex character of the man.   This pre-eminently is the proper field for the psychologist of history, the lover of strange souls and mingled motives; for we have groaned too long under the affliction of those who would leave historical portraiture to the mere romancer or crush a manifold personality into the bounds of a narrow theory.   But in these pages we set before ourselves a more modest task.   It were needless to enter into the minutiae of evidence on which the narrative is founded. The facts of his life have already been ascertained with tolerable certainty by more competent scholars, and there is little need for an amateur's vain repetition. We would seek rather to sketch his character roughly and crudely, to trace the war of motive which at all times beset him; to find, in short, in his temper and talents some explanation of the cruel circumstances of his fate.

II.

By the end of the sixteenth century the family of Ralegh had held lands in the west of England for upwards of three hundred years, and in Devonshire had won a position of power among the gentry of the country-side. There were several families of the name, all men of good repute, allied to the Champernouns, the Carews, and the Gilberts, and other houses of renown in the place. At the manor of Hayes, near the town of Budleigh Salterton, lived Walter Ralegh of Hayes and Fardell, who married as his third wife Katherine Champernoun, the widow of Sir Otho Gilbert of Compton. Of this union two sons were born, Carew and Walter.

Of the father we hear little save that he suffered in the Catholic rising[1] in the west, and that he was forced by straitened circumstances to sell one of the family manors. But we can make a guess at the manner of upbringing which the young Walter would share in. He came of a fighting stock and a godly, so he would be trained in all martial exercises and bred in the strict tenets of the Protestantism of his time. But to one born in Devonshire there fell a richer boyhood than to the rest of England. The rule of Mary in its season fell less hardly there, and the accession

[1] Holinshed, *Chronicles of England*, continued by Hooker, anno 1549.

of Elizabeth soon brought the needful hope and liberty.
Religious ardour was subtly mixed with the desire of adventure and the sea; the land was full of tales—the distorted
traditions of an oppressed sect on the eve of freedom as
well as the legends of the marvellous ocean. Spain was
already a hated name; but the stories of Spanish adventure
were the first which kindled the ardent spirits of the time.
Cortes still lived, and the tale of his deeds would be known
to many. Englishmen themselves had made like voyages,
had seen like wonders, had shown like daring. Living not
far from the coast, he could scarcely fail to hear the sailor-
tales of the coastmen, who were the hardiest and stoutest of
their kind in the land. All such influences would make for
high spirit and large intentions, also for a certain bragga-
docio eagerness which we never find wholly absent from
Ralegh the man.

In what year he went to Oriel, when he left it, and how
long thereafter he remained in France, we have no certain
information. It is probable that the year 1567 first saw
him at Oxford, and that early in 1569 he left for the French
wars. We know few details of his university life. A stray
apophthegm of Bacon's[1] makes him the author of a pointless
repartee; and Anthony Wood[2] tells us that 'his natural
gifts being strangely advanced by academical learning, under
the care of an excellent tutor, he became the ornament of
the juniors, and was worthily esteemed a proficient in
Oratory and Philosophy.' It was necessary, indeed, that
one of Ralegh's vigorous and adaptable mind should make
something of a college reputation; but it was impossible
that such a one could settle down to any academical groove
when the whole land was already in a ferment of military
zeal. To one of so many talents, learning must have
seemed but a little one of the joys of life, and many years

---

[1] Bacon, *Apophthegms*, LXVI.
[2] *Athenae Oxonienses*, ii. 235.

had to elapse ere scholarship again claimed her own. Of his French career, as far as authentic records go, we know little more. It seems tolerably certain that he made one of a troop which his kinsman Henry Champernoun raised to assist the Huguenots. We know that he was present at Moncontour, and that he possibly made one of the small English band in Paris on the Eve of St. Bartholomew. The reason for this lack of knowledge is to be traced to the secret and illicit nature of such warfare, waged as it was with the connivance, but against the public command of the Queen. From Hakluyt we know with fair certainty the date of his return, in 1576, when he had already reached his twenty-fifth year.

The record of such a training is varied enough, and forms something of an index to the versatility of his manhood. A hardy boyhood, two years of quiet study, and then a sudden immersion in the full tide of guerilla warfare, may fairly leave their stamp upon character. In him they doubtless developed that shrewdness in affairs, energy in action, and wide knowledge of men which distinguished his after career. The short years of his Oxford life may be supposed to have laid the seeds of something still more valuable to his successors—that varied learning and power to write well and wisely which would alone have made his name worthy of memory.

III.

With his return, we pass at once from guesswork to a record of action based upon reliable authority. The Irish campaigns may be considered the real beginning of his career, since there for the first time an opportunity was given for the full and independent exercise of his talents. Ireland for long had been the *corpus vile* on which each new statesman exercised his untried powers and the young soldier his prowess. Its condition was curious and unhappy. A country of a thousand sects and clanships, it had originally been conquered only in name. The invaders had sunk to the condition of the invaded; Bourkes and Fitzgeralds were in no way different from M'Carthies and O'Neills; and centuries of internal warfare ensued, unchecked by the feeble rule of the Lord Deputy at Dublin. The various measures of subjugation served only to increase the discontent. It was useless to legislate in one way for the degenerate English and in another for the Irish chieftains, when both were in the bonds of a common interest. Around the coast there were many oases of peace and prosperity, such as the eighth Earl of Desmond created at Youghal, where a seat of learning existed and commerce flourished. It is easy to paint the state of Ireland in colours too black in order to heighten the expediency of the English remedy. The country was no worse than any other land where a strong clan system is more than a match for the central power. But the fact was only too apparent to every thinking Englishman of the time that, in its present condition, the country lay open to Spanish intrigues and was a dangerous neighbour to any nation. For the great evil there was but one remedy. In some way or other it was necessary that the strength of the great native houses should be broken and the land made subservient to an English government. Apart from the constitutional danger, the rule of the chiefs was not seldom mere rapine and injustice. The conservative feeling of the most conservative nation in the world made the poorer folk cling to the last to their oppressors; but the feeling was no more than sentimental, and if peace and justice were to exist in the land they could only be found under the English power.

The only question on which opinion could divide was as to the precise nature of this subjugation. Could such a result be brought about gradually and peaceably with the smallest use of military force, or was the swift sharp remedy of extermination the only one possible? At this later day it is easy for us who have learned the lesson of the years to decide at once for the former, and talk wisely of the inevitable reaction which follows violence and the folly of neglecting national spirit. But to the men of that time no such considerations were present. They had before them a great difficulty which clamoured for immediate and final settlement; time did not permit of fine theories or humane experiments; the crisis needed a resolute and unflinching hand. So argued the Greys, Spensers, and Raleghs; so also at a later date the Mountjoys, Carews, and Chichesters. There was one further side to the question. Ireland was a Roman Catholic country where it was not pagan; her ablest men were priests; so there entered into the war something of the bitterness of religious strife. The existence of the Catholic Church in the eyes of the English captains was incompatible with the material prosperity of any land; so, if for no other reason than this, a war of extermination must be waged.

In such a tempest of affairs Ralegh entered upon his work. It seems probable, from various pieces of evidence, that he was first engaged in a small sea-venture with Sir Humphrey Gilbert[1], and it may even be assumed that he saw something of the war in the Netherlands. At any rate, we find him in Cork in the February of 1580, with a small band of well-trained soldiers, chiefly from his native Devonshire. Two years later Captain Appesley's band fell to him, but at no time was his force large. The English of that day, as Ralegh[2] himself is careful to explain, owed their easy victories over huge Irish hordes to their superior arms and lusty condition.

---

[1] *Register Book of the Privy Council: Elizabeth*, vol. iv.

[2] 'Discourse touching a War with Spain,' *Works*, vol. viii. pp. 304, 305.

On the many details of his campaigns it is unnecessary to enter. We hear of his presence at the condemnation of James Earl of Desmond. At Rakele he laid an ambush and won a moderate victory, and shortly after we find him remonstrating with Lord Grey himself on certain errors of policy. He was high in favour with the Deputy and Council at Dublin, and was given a free hand in his work. We hear of extraordinary gallantry shown at a ford between Youghal and Cork, when, in the face of an Irish force, he risked his life to save a soldier, fighting with pistol and quarter-staff, one against twenty. But the two incidents in his career which stand out most strongly are his capture of Lord Roche and his share in the slaughter at Smerwick. In the first, he boldly surprised the rebel lord in his house of Bally, arrested him, and, in spite of the continuous hostile ambuscades, succeeded in conveying his prisoner to Lord Ormond's camp. The act was brilliant in plan and execution, but into it, as into all his Irish exploits, there enters a tinge of treachery and false faith. The second has given rise to endless defences and diatribes, all agreeing in condemning the details, but many defending the policy. The fort of Smerwick was besieged by Grey on land and Sir William Winter on sea. After two summonses to surrender, on the third day 'Captain Ralegh and Captain M'Worth entered into the castle and made a great slaughter,' in spite of the fact that the rebels hung out a white flag and cried for mercy. Six hundred at least—men, women, and children—were slain, stripped, and laid out upon the sands [1].

It is very easy to condemn such an act unsparingly, and let humanitarian considerations play havoc with fact. The deed was no unconsidered butchery, but the result of a definite policy of annihilation, adopted in some degree

---

[1] Hooker's *Supplement to Holinshed.*

by all the captains then in the Irish service. Again, very many of the massacred were the offscourings of Italian prisons, liberated by the Pope expressly to serve in the Irish wars. It was hardly to be expected that much mercy should be shown to these. Yet the fact of its unspeakable cold-blooded cruelty remains, and we may safely discredit Camden's story of Grey's tears and Elizabeth's sighs and regrets. Two letters from the Queen herself are preserved among the State Papers, in the first of which she calls the deed 'this so acceptable a service to us,' and in the second describes it as 'the great good services done us chiefly in the late exployt against the strayngers that had invaded the realms, for the which we do carrye a thanckfull remembraunce[1].'

Ralegh's share in the matter is less worthy of consideration than his relation to the policy of which this was an outcome. It is necessary to examine the view which he took of the condition of the land and its possible remedy, for on this must rest in part our view of his character. What the current policy was we have already stated. The Irish clan-system must be broken at any cost, the people must be wholly brought under subjection, and the land must fall into the hands of Englishmen and native lords of approved loyalty, with the native population, greatly reduced in number, working as labourers under severe disabilities. To attain this lofty end all means were permissible—wholesale butchery, assassination, and treachery. Such practices were sanctioned by the Queen and carried on by the Lord Deputy himself. The O'Neills and Desmonds were plotted against with the utmost pertinacity by successive captains. It is certain from existing correspondence that Elizabeth was aware of such attempts and still continued the Greys and Sussexes in office. Cecil, as may be inferred from

[1] Sir J. Pope-Hennessy's *Ralegh in Ireland*, Appendix, pp. 214, 215.

a letter of Ralegh's, looked askance at the state of affairs, and it is clear that Burghley disapproved. 'The Flemings,' he wrote to Sir Henry Wallop, 'had not such cause to rebel against the oppression of the Spaniards as the Irish against the tyranny of England[1].' He directed that confiscated lands should be given not to persons, but to offices. He saw the result which must follow from this criminally foolish policy of murder and fraud; but he was almost alone in his time, and all his efforts were met and counteracted by Irish officials. Nor was the feeling of the English nation at the time otherwise than in favour of this *régime* of 'Thorough,' for Ireland was still too little known and too much suspected to be an object for interest or pity.

In all this we know that Ralegh played an active part. His feelings in the matter differed in no way from those of the hundreds of English gentlemen who learned their trade in those desultory wars. We might indeed suppose that his action was only a soldier's obedience to orders, did we not know that his hand was practically free. There remain, too, some letters in which he gives an explicit account of his policy. One to Sir Robert Cecil is a defence of the practice of assassination. 'It can be no disgrace,' writes this model of chivalry, 'if it were known that the killinge of a rebel were practised; for you see that the lives of anoynted princes are daylye sought, and we have always in Ireland geven head money for the killinge of rebels who ar ever-more proclaymed at a price.' Again, he writes to Sir Francis Walsingham[2], complaining bitterly of the unnecessary mildness of Ormond's rule. 'I would to God,' he cries, 'that he looked more to the service of Sir Humphrey Gilbert.' What the service of Sir Humphrey was we may learn from a letter of his own to Sir Henry Sidney: 'After my first summoning of a castle or fort, if they would not

---

[1] Froude, *History of England*, x. p. 64.
[2] *Irish Correspondence: Elizabeth*, vol. lxxx. § 82.

presently yield it, I would not thereafter take it of their
gift, but won it perforce—how many lives soever it cost;
putting man, woman, and child of them to the sword.'

From this two questions arise, which we may find it hard
to answer :—How could a man of Ralegh's stamp go through
such a catalogue of horrors without leaving us one hint of
sympathy with the distressed or compunction at the use
of such a method; and how came it that one who in after
years was wise politically beyond most of his generation
should have given countenance to so ruinous a policy ?
From his subsequent history we can learn something of
a sensitiveness bordering on the sentimental, and a tender-
ness of heart unusual to a man of his life. How comes it
then that the note of sorrow which rings through Spenser's
State of Ireland, when the tale is told of the thin, white
faces of the peasants, dying for lack of food, looking with
blind eyes on the places which had once been their home
—how comes it that all this is absent from Ralegh's schemes
and letters ? Again, how does it happen that one who
showed in most things such far-sighted wisdom, who in
time to come wrote down political maxims whose truth we
still acknowledge, gave his sanction, aye, and his best energies, to the depopulation of Irish land, and the repeopling
with English settlers? In some of the details even of his
Irish labours he showed good sense and penetration. In
a memorandum of Lord Burghley's Ralegh's opinions on
the forces to be kept in Munster[1] are noted, in which he
argues for the necessity of winning over some of the minor
Irish chieftains, and gives his reasons with admirable shrewdness. How then is his Irish career, in spite of its brilliance
and gallantry, one long and dismal error ?

We can give but one answer to the question. When
a man in whom humane sentiment runs high forswears his

---

[1] Hennessy, *Ralegh in Ireland*, Appendix xvi.

gods and shuts off his pity, when a rational and far-seeing
politician lends himself to a policy the most short-sighted
and futile, we can only attribute it to the expulsive power of
a stronger interest. The temper of the soldiers and adven-
turers, Ralegh among the rest, who have given so great
a glory to the age of Elizabeth, was fine gold compounded
with much clay. Scarcely one of their more absorbing
motives was wholly pure. In all there was a nervous desire
to attain honour, wealth, and power, a lust of adventure
and excitement, a hatred of slow monotonous toil, a passion
for the swift, glittering methods of success. We can con-
ceive Ralegh as not at first without his scruples, moral and
intellectual. But all were soon choked by his triumphant
egotism. The way to success lay in bold unscrupulousness,
and this way had the sanction of all. Conscious of great
powers and fierce energies, he flung himself forthwith into
the struggle for name and wealth, and came out victorious.
Fame he got, and wealth which he was not destined to
enjoy long. Before passing from these years of Irish life,
their remain for consideration Ralegh's commercial schemes
and territorial acquisitions.

We find him in 1581 writing to Sir Francis Walsingham
and asking for the estate of Barry's Court at Queenstown,
which from its nearness to the sea was especially pleasant
to one who was no less sailor than soldier. On the Black-
water he had no less than forty-two thousand acres of richly
wooded country, so that he was already a proprietor of some
importance. To these estates he brought his Devonshire
farmers, and the band of Englishmen set themselves patiently
to the task of cultivating the neglected land. The Irishry
were pressed into the service first by promises and then by
threats. But with it all we find incessant complaints in
Ralegh's letters of the hardships of his task, the obstinacy
of the peasants, and the folly of the Government at Dublin
Castle. The land question was as perplexing a problem to

Ralegh as to his late successors, and we read of his many schemes for amelioration with a feeling of the pathetic hopelessness of it all. He failed grievously, as all must fail who seek to rule a people of which they are ignorant by force of the sword.

Indeed, through the whole history of his life as an Irish landowner there runs a very ugly thread of desire for wealth. We do not find him hesitating to share in the spoils of the Geraldine College at Youghal, though to a man of his liberal culture we might have assumed that letters would appear above the reach of military oppression. Again, he did not scruple to follow the disastrous English custom of cutting down the fine Irish woods to serve his own purposes. George Longe [1], in 1588, asked Lord Burghley to transfer thirteen English glass manufactories to Ireland, that the Irish woods, 'the harbour of the rebels,' might be put to some use. But Ralegh has no other aim than money-making. He brought over English woodcutters, obtained a monopoly for exporting wine-staves abroad, and furnished hogsheads for the export to England of French, Spanish, and Italian wines. The scheme was not uniformly prosperous. We find in many subsequent letters and papers, notes of lawsuits, petitions, and quarrels with the Government. But the whole affair is significant of the active spirit which gave it birth, as well as the singular commercial and utilitarian strain in a character otherwise tending to the quixotic.

But meantime his affairs prospered in another quarter, and preparations were being made for his entrance into a very different life. We can see from the published correspondence of the time how his influence with the Queen had grown during these years. In a letter of 1582 to the Lord Deputy she specially mentions him. In 1587 he is 'our well-beloved Sir Walter Rawley.' He is placed first

---

[1] Ellis, *Original Letters*, iii. p. 159.

in the list of Irish captains, and served as one of the six
in the Royal Commission against Tyrone[1]. Naunton has
a story that it was owing to a dispute with Lord Grey
before the Queen and Council that Elizabeth's attention
was first drawn to the young soldier; but whether or not
we accept this it seems clear that toward the end of his
service he had risen high in favour. We find a new captain's commission made out for him in the April of 1582,
but it seems probable that when he left Cork with the Lord
Deputy's dispatches in December, 1581, he closed his Irish
service. He returned to England with something of a
reputation and good recommendations at Court, which, with
a handsome presence and pleasing discourse, were destined
to carry him far. He never again returned to the country
in an official capacity, and in 1602 he sold almost all his
Irish estate to Richard Boyle, afterwards Earl of Cork. But
his advice was sought on Irish questions, and we find
him, still true to his old maxim of 'Thorough,' vigorously
opposing the gentler policy of Essex.

IV.

We have already seen in some measure the character of
Ralegh at this new turn in the tide of his fortunes. A man
of unshaken self-confidence, bold, hardy, and in the main
self-seeking, he was possessed of a capacity for influencing
men and gifts of mind far in advance of the majority of his
rivals. Even his faults were brilliant—his impatience, his
love of the bizarre and coloured in life, his extravagance,
his intolerance of mediocrity. Leicester was the leading
figure of the time at Court, and Ralegh soon became
associated with him as a claimant for the Queen's favour.
It is probable that the two had already met in France; at.

---

[1] Hennessy, *Ralegh in Ireland*, pp. 31, 32.

any rate no violent enmity ever arose between them, however much their partisans may have bickered among themselves. The Queen's affection was wide enough to admit of two.

It is needless to enter at length into the string of brilliant exaggerations which with Elizabeth did duty for character. It is easy to recognize her uncommon ability, and to form a tolerably accurate conception of her passionate temper, her violence in love and hatred, her liking for dramatic effect, her mania for the gorgeous, her woman's petulance fighting ever with a more than statesmanlike sagacity. Her Court was a place of tournaments and shows, a house of wit and brave display. We can well understand how this would fall in with the tastes of the young soldier fresh from moorland wars; how his handsome face and port, joined to his growing fame, would soon win for him first notice, then admission to the inner circle of the palace, and finally more substantial tokens of favour. The tincture of letters which pervaded the Royal society would give a further opportunity to one who, like Ralegh, was always a scholar and friend of scholars.

We have an accurate record of the growth of his fortunes in the list of grants enumerated in the *Domestic Correspondence*. He had various licences to export broadcloth, from which the profits, as calculated by Burghley, were very high[1]. He had a grant of the ' Farm of Wines,' and the consequent power of granting licences. These gifts were not unattended with trouble, but there is no doubt about the size of the resulting income. In 1585 he was made Lord Warden of the Stannaries in succession to the Earl of Bedford; in the same year Lieutenant of Cornwall, and soon afterwards Vice-Admiral of Cornwall and Devon. In 1587 he became Captain of the Queen's Guard, a post in which his passion for display would have full vent.

---

[1] *Domestic Correspondence : Elizabeth,* vol. ccxxix. § 101.

Finally, on the discovery of Babington's conspiracy he was gifted with nearly all the forfeited property, and became a large landowner in several counties. Times were indeed changed with one who a little before had been toiling in the bogs of Munster.

It is unnecessary to linger long over the history of these years. It is the history of multifarious duties well performed, for Ralegh could 'toil' both 'terribly' and to good purpose, of difficulties surmounted, of dazzling leaps into high place. But the man is not at his best. His great powers of body and mind needed fuller vent than the narrow round of Court ceremonial could afford. With all his faults we feel that if he could not be a great statesman, he was too much of the man to sink into the mere courtier. But two incidents deserve notice ere we turn to more stirring years. One is the rise of the young Lord Essex, and the beginning of the long game which was to end so disastrously. The other is the visit of the little Lady Arabella Stuart to Court as a child of twelve, when she met Ralegh at supper and the names of the two were coupled in jest by her uncle, Sir Charles Cavendish. Years after the same conjunction was to bring forth dismal fruits for both.

V.

Two causes led to the maritime exploits which make so large a feature in Ralegh's history. One was his unconquerable hatred of Spain, bred in his bone as a boy in Devonshire, fostered by sailor-tales and the French wars, kindled fiercer by the facts of the Munster rebellion and the difficulties of his Irish policy. But it was more than a local prejudice or a dislike founded on the accidents of fortune; it was a firm, well-grounded belief that the interests of the Spanish nation and of his own were eternally at variance, that the Great Monarch represented all that was most opposed to that intellectual, religious, and civil freedom which was dear to his heart. The other was his belief in colonization as a national policy. No man of his ardent nature could fail to be roused to enthusiasm by the voyages of the Gilberts and the Drakes to the West. The dream of a great country beyond the sea, peopled with the English race, an offshoot and ally of England, was ever before him. He had already made some trial of colonizing schemes on his land in Ireland, but there they had failed from opposition which could not be met with in that newer world. It does credit to his statesmanship that his dreams of conquest were always based on colonization. Order, government, participation in some greater whole, were the things he sought in his Utopias.

It is remarkable that his period of naval activity should be so closely associated with the luxury of his Court life. It seems to point to the craving of some part of his nature which found no satisfaction in pageant and diplomacy. He had always something of that love of the free face of heaven, the salt wind, and the fierce delight of action, which is the glory of his race. Over him and his like the old glamour of the 'swan's path' had fallen in all its power. He and men of his kind at the very height of achievement in other spheres seem always weary for the sting of wind and rain and the ecstasy of motion. And for them in their toils there was a richer hope than for others of the craft in later times. For the world was not yet shorn and parcelled; treasure might still be looked for, portents awaited, and the white harbour-wall of the Devon town was the boundary of the unknown.

Sir Humphrey Gilbert had obtained a royal charter in the year 1578, licensing him to 'hereafter discover such remote heathen and barbarous lands not actually possessed of any Christian prince or people.' Ralegh was eager to join his half-brother, but was prevented by the Council, now grown

timid over ceaseless Spanish complaints. To the expense
of that last and memorable expedition, which cost its gallant
leader his life, he advanced £2,000. As soon as the tragic
result was known in England, Ralegh assumed command,
and obtained a new charter from the Queen, 'admitting him
to the College of the Fellowship of the North-West Passage.'
The direct outcome of the undertaking was the discovery
and attempted colonization of the land to which he gave
the name of Virginia, he himself, as the seal of his arms
relates, being *dominus et gubernator Virginiae*. He laboured
incessantly on behalf of the new colony, sending out
a fleet of seven sail under Sir Richard Grenville, with
a hundred householders on board to form the nucleus of
the new state. A series of mischances all but nipped the
undertaking in the bud. All the first crew soon fell sick of
their task and were taken by Sir Francis Drake to England.
Their successors quarrelled among themselves, and fell easy
victims to the native arrows. From 1587 to 1602 it seems
probable that Ralegh fitted out five separate expeditions
entirely at his own expense. At one time his hopes fell so
low that he leased out his patent to a merchant company in
the hope that public credit might succeed where private
resources failed. In every vicissitude of his own fortunes
he kept his interest fresh in the struggling colony oversea.
'I shall yet live to see it in an English nation,' was ever his
comforting watchword.

In all this there is a mingling of motives. It is unlikely
that the graver considerations on the subject of such
enterprises, which he afterwards entertained in his enforced
retirement at Sherborne, were present in those early
experiments. He was not yet fired with the great dream of
an English America wider than any Spanish possessions, of
England as the protectress of the native races, leading them
upward to civilization and law. With that curious note of
political sagacity which was never quite absent from his

speculations, he regarded the lands as the home of peoples
and not the common ground of plunder. Nay, he went
further; he saw England enriched and strengthened by
such allies, righting the wrongs of Europe and leading the
van of the nations of the earth. But now his motive was
probably more personal and boyish. He was still in the
flush of young enthusiasm when a man's vanity prompts
him to admit of no obstacles in his course. The love for
display, for the rhetorical in word and design, had much
sway over his heart. It pleased him to think of himself
as not only the successful soldier and the accomplished
courtier, but as a pioneer in unknown places, a founder of
nations, at once a lawgiver and a captain. Yet we may
admit some such feeling to be the ruling motive and not
discredit others. The plain physical love of the sea and
the open air went for much; and there are not wanting
hints of that genuine love of country and his country's
greatness which redeems all, and that power of sound
political thinking, which was only prevented by his
subsequent misfortunes from realization in action.

The other side of his naval activity is to be found in his
hostility towards Spain, his share in the Armada, and his
subsequent buccaneering reprisals. His hatred of Spanish
claims may be traced to his Devon ancestry and upbringing, and to those qualities in his nature which at all
times were the most prominent—a love of liberty and
a vigorous enlightened nation of freemen. Through all the
intrigues and counter-intrigues which marked the early reign
of Elizabeth's successor, he preserved the same uncompromising aversion to anything which savoured of Spain. In
the two *Discourses on the Marriage of Prince Henry*[1], which
he wrote in the Tower, we find his scorn poured on the class
which with some felicity he called 'Englishmen Hispaniol-
ized.' And this dislike, as we have said, had more in it

[1] *Works*, vol. viii. (Oxford ed.) p. 236.

than mere prejudice or natural antipathy.   At the root
of all his political theories lay the conviction, based on
rational grounds, that if England were to maintain her
place and enlarge her coasts it must be in the teeth of
Spanish resistance.   We need not inquire too closely into
the question whether or not such a belief has had historical
justification.   Many new factors were to come to light
after Ralegh's day had passed, which gave the matter
another aspect.   But it is certain that his view was shared
by some of the wisest of his time, and, starting from
the facts which were known to him, it seems the only
possible.

As soon as the news of the Armada came to him, Ralegh
hastened with what speed he might to Devon and Cornwall,
made considerable levies, and, as governor, increased the
fortifications of Portland Island.   It was not till July 23
that he joined the fleet—two days after the actual
commencement of the fight.   Of Ralegh's part in it we
know little more than that in popular belief he was well to
the front [1], and is credited with having advised the admiral,
Lord 'Howard, to refrain from the folly of grappling.   At
any rate he has left us a record of his detestation of the
practice, and as an instance where its use would have been
fatal he cites this very scene [2].   We are not yet in possession
of a full account of the reprisals which followed, but we can
make a tolerable estimate of the part Ralegh played.   He
fitted out several ships and sent them to sea ; they did
havoc among all and sundry ; and the result is that we find
many suits in the Admiralty Courts on the subject of these

---

[1] I have followed the ordinary tradition in ascribing to Ralegh
a share in the Armada's defeat, but the only apparent authority is the
extremely doubtful ' Copie of a letter sent out of England to Don
Bernardin Mendoza, 1588,' where the obvious mistake is made of
attributing a like share to Cecil.

[2] *Hist. of World*, v. chap. i. § 6.

expeditions[1]. He also bore a part in Drake's fruitless voyage to Portugal, but it is unlikely that he had any say in the management. In various enterprises he had money embarked, and we find records of sums paid to him for the sale of prizes. In all this there is something of the money-lover, something of the pure soldier, and something of the courtier. He seeks to add to his fortune, but he has always his glance on the Queen, and his mind is constantly on the figure he makes in that critical eye. But he has also something of the ready pleasure in mere action, tempered with gleams of insight and fragments of political projects. At this juncture, in short, he is still the man of varied and distinguished talents, who has raised himself to prominence, but has not yet found an absorbing activity.

VI.

The next years of his life are filled with a record of quarrels with the Queen, of labours undertaken in the teeth of difficulties, and of the growth of his rivalry with the young Earl of Essex. In 1589 we find him from no apparent cause retiring to Ireland and living with Spenser at Kilcolman. *Colin Clout's come home again* was the result, and we know not what effect this short stay had on the production of the slender stock of poetry which the 'Shepherd of the Ocean' has left us. We know that he gave the poet much help and encouragement in the writing of the *Faerie Queene*, and on his return won something of royal favour for its author. Soon we find Ralegh again at Court, extending a hand of help to the Puritan Udall, and sharing the protectorate of that party with Essex, who is supposed by many to have been the cause of his previous

---

[1] Edwards' *Ralegh*, vol. ii. pp. 55 sqq. *Register of the Privy Council: Elizabeth*, vol. viii. Part I. p. 212, also vol. xi. pp. 57, 70, 71.

retirement. In all the history of those early relations between the two favourites there is something unintelligible. At one moment they are at drawn daggers, engaged to fight a mortal duel, at the next they are coadjutors in some scheme or companions in misfortune.

The latter was soon to be the fate of both, for in 1592 Ralegh by his marriage with Elizabeth Throgmorton roused the same wrath in the Queen which Essex had stirred up two years before by his marriage with Frances Walsingham. The lady was a maid of honour, and her seduction, and still more her marriage, roused Elizabeth's deepest resentment. The breach of the special royal virtue in the maid seemed almost a slur upon the Queen ; and the resulting marriage was doubly bitter to one who loved the presence of handsome young men with unmaidenly ardour. The character of Lady Ralegh is one of the most attractive in the whole history of the times. A strong, brave woman, full of honesty and good sense, endowed with a fair face and a valiant temper, she was at all times a fitting companion to her husband ; and her courage and gentleness shone forth the more brightly in the darkest hour of his fortunes. 'I chose you and I loved you in my happiest times,' wrote Ralegh long afterwards, and rarely has choice been more justified or love better deserved.

The result of the affair was his instant dismissal from favour and imprisonment in the Tower. At no time did he appear to less advantage. The strain of rhetoric, which was never far absent from his nature, led him into wild extravaganzas. He fought with his keepers and bemoaned himself to the grim Sir Robert Cecil. 'I, that was wont to behold her riding like Alexander, hunting like Diana, walking like Venus; the gentle air blowing her fair hair about her pure cheeks like a nymph ; sometime, sitting in the shade like a goddess ; sometime, singing like an angel ; sometime, playing like Orpheus. All these times past—the

loves, the sighs, the sorrows, the desires.' But no dithy-
rambics could relax the frown of the stony-hearted goddess ;
and we have the unedifying spectacle of this gentleman and
scholar descending into the lackadaisical clown.

His solitary meditations were first broken in upon by the
royal command to go down to Dartmouth to assist in the
division of the Spanish spoils. An expedition under
Lord Thomas Howard and Ralegh had been planned in
1591, but on account of the pressure of his Warden's work,
Ralegh had to send Sir Richard Grenville in his stead.
The result was the Thermopylae of our English history,
when Grenville in his own ship the *Revenge* kept fifteen
Spanish ships at bay for fifteen hours, and fell himself with
words on his lips like a Viking's war-song. In the greater
expedition of 1592 Ralegh was prohibited by the Queen's
express command from sharing to the full ; the reason at
first probably being mere anxiety for a favourite, and then
anger at his offence. But he had sufficient share in the
matter to make the attempt a brilliant success. The
Madre de Dios, one of the greatest of the Indian galleons,
was taken, and, with her, treasures that surpassed all hopes.
England was flooded with foreign money and foreign goods,
and Sir Robert Cecil, with his family love of the lion's share,
rode post haste to the west to superintend the distribution.

In all this Ralegh was incapacitated from benefiting by
the ban of the Queen's displeasure. He naturally grew
restive at the silly caprice which deprived the nation of the
services of the one man most fitted to rule in the matter.
Nor were his sailors in a better frame of mind at the
reported disgrace of their captain. It soon became evident
that there could be no settlement till Ralegh was summoned
to help. Accordingly Lord Burghley obtained permission
for his journey to the west with a keeper as befitted a
prisoner of state. Few things show better the affection
which the man's personality could inspire than the letter

of Sir Robert Cecil's which tells of the welcome Ralegh received. 'I assure you, Sir, his poor servants to the number of a hundred and forty goodly men, and all the mariners, came to him with such shouts and joy, as I never saw a man more troubled to quell them in my life. But his heart is broken; for he is very extreme pensive longer than he is busied, in which he can toil terribly [1].'

The sharing of the spoils was another drop in the cup of Ralegh's grievances. The Queen's greed made the division extremely unequal, and to the poor projectors of the enterprise there fell a very small share indeed. Lord Cumberland made £17,000 of profit on his venture; Ralegh, to whom the success was owing, who bore the toils and burden of it all, was considerably the loser. His money losses may not command our sympathy, for as he had risen to affluence by royal favour, so also he might look to fall. But the circumstances of his imprisonment and the galling hindrances set in the way of his free action at a time when he was most eager to serve his country, had something in them peculiarly irksome to his restless mind. His anti-Spanish policy may have been little better than free piracy, but at any rate we can understand his feelings at its frustration.

There is no precise information on the date of his release from imprisonment; but we find him early in 1593 in retirement at the manor of Sherborne in Dorset. Freedom from confinement did not bring with it a return of the royal graciousness, and for some years he was practically an exile from the Court. Of the way in which he spent his time of leisure we have some information, and can guess the rest. The mere delights of country life occupied him much, and to the aforetime man of many toils the pleasant woods and gardens were a haven of content. He busied himself with building and planting after the regal fashion of the

[1] *Domestic Correspondence: Elizabeth*, September, 1592.

courtier in retirement, and made the place dear to him with
a thousand devices and improvements of his own.   Perhaps
he returned to his early love of poetry, and

> 'took in hand
> The pipe—before that emuléd of many—
> And played thereon (for well that skill he conned);
> Himself as skilful in the art as any.'

Of one pursuit we know from after results.   The records
of the early navigators, English and Spanish, the narrative
of the first Hakluyt, the histories of Alfinger and Perez de
Quesada, of von Hutten and Pedro de Ursua, would be
his constant study.   The present failure of his courtiership
would lead a man of his nature to a more eager search for
new activities, where his hand might be free and the work
demand his best talent.   He turned instinctively to the
domain of naval enterprise.   It seems probable from a letter
of Lady Ralegh's to Cecil[1] that thoughts of a new expedition in search of El Dorado were occupying his attention.
'We poor souls,' she writes with genuine entreaty, 'that
have bought sorrow at a high price, desire, and can be
pleased with the same misfortunes we hold; fearing altera-
tions will but multiply miseries.   I know only your per-
suasions are of effect with him, and held as oracles tied
together by love.   Therefore, I humbly beseech you, rather
stay him than further him.'   But whatever the date at which
the desire came upon him, we know that with the months
it grew to a great resolution.   All his mingled hopes of
colonization, conquest, and personal aggrandisement were
joined to a desire to increase the national welfare; and to
all were added a thirst for sudden fame, and the delight
of the imagination in perhaps the most romantic quest
mankind has ever sought.   It is easy at this time of day to
laugh at those dreams of a Golden City, and explain the

[1] *Cecil Papers*, vol. xxii. § 50.

fabled lake of Parima by the floods of the Orinoco, and the story of precious metals by the mica in the rocks.   But to Ralegh and his contemporaries incredulity in the matter' was almost inconceivable.   The glamour of the poetic and the marvellous made expeditions, seeking no more than piracy or ordinary commerce, seem noble to the eyes of all men of imagination.   We can well understand how Ralegh among his Dorset fields would grow sick once more for action and the sea, and look to the Guiana expedition as the satisfaction of all that was best in his nature and least sordid in his aims.

But it is reasonable to ask at this juncture what Ralegh sought in his multifarious plans.   The probability is that he was content to go on realizing the demands which a singularly energetic nature made without seeking to combine all to some great end.   It may indeed have been that at one time he sought to attain such a place in statesmanship as Burghley held and Cecil afterwards won, and that the hostility of the old Lord Treasurer and the coldness of the son can be explained by such a clashing of interests.   But if such a scheme ever entered Ralegh's mind it did not long keep its place.   It was one of the defects in his character that he could never abide the monotonous, that he was incapable of dogged, persistent struggling through the arduous and the dull to an appointed end.   We may explain it by a certain largeness of mind, which set mere rewards in their proper light, and preferred to strive rather than to attain.   But we are immediately confronted with the fact that he loved in an exceptional degree the luxuries and pomps of life.   Yet something of this magnanimity is to be found, if not in conscious purpose, at least in the nature of the man at his better moments.   He was at his happiest in work when he had no prize held before him.   He found reward in the mere exercise of magnificent gifts; and we shall not err in saying that to him versatility was an end in itself, and a hundred little successes dearer than supreme power. It is the defect of a generous nature, and, as his intellectual keynote, does much to explain future inconsistencies of word and deed.

VII.

The details of the first and most successful Guiana expedition are happily made plain to us by Ralegh's own narrative. In 1594 a certain Captain Whiddon was sent as pioneer to Trinidad, where the governor, De Berreo, put such obstacles in his way that he returned with little information. On Feb. 9, 1595, Sir Walter himself set sail from Plymouth, bound for the same port. He arrived about the end of March, after some piracy on the high seas by which he increased his slender equipment. He at once laid hands on Berreo, and proceeded to conciliate the Indian inhabitants and learn the details of Orinoco navigation. Meantime the governor's lieutenant, De Vera, had gone on a mission to Spain to collect funds for a new Spanish exploration of Guiana. The floating rumours of treasure and El Dorados had been carefully gathered by the Spaniards, and were magnified into astounding declarations with which the people of Seville were roused to the same fever of expectancy. The result was that De Vera set out from home with ample supplies and liberal grants of prerogative. There is evidence that Ralegh himself was shown some of the more wonderful proofs of the great unknown land which lay beyond the trackless forests—particularly that strange story of Juan Martinez, which told how he was led blindfolded by Indian captors to the city of Manoa the Golden, and found it so mighty that he entered the gates at noon and did not reach the palace of the king till the evening of the next day. All this was so much fresh fuel to the already kindled fire of enterprise,

and it was with new zeal that the small English crew
embarked on their perilous boat-voyage on the Orinoco.

Of the full hardships of such a journey we can guess
better from the reports of later explorers than the simple
narrative of Ralegh. They first crossed a piece of sea
as large as that between Dover and Calais with a great
tempest blowing in their teeth. Then came the terrible
rowing of several hundred miles against a powerful current.
They were fortunate enough at the outset to capture an
Indian pilot who knew the tortuous maze of channels
and tributaries. Their chief afflictions were the frequent
shallows, the sudden and terrible floodings when the
stream swept on them 'like a mountain,' and the constant
exposure to heat and cold. By day the thick woods shut
in the air and the rowers fainted at their tasks ; the banks
were so dense with thickets that at night they were often
unable to land, and had to endure the heavy dews of
a tropical darkness under no shelter. At last, as the
glowing narrative tells us, the black forests ceased, and
they came out into a pleasant country of far-stretching
meadows and green woods, as at home in England, while
the shy deer looked mildly at them from the water's edge.

Finally, they arrived at the dwelling of an old chief
Topiawari, whose nephew had been put to death by
Berreo. He gladly welcomed Ralegh as an enemy of
Spain, and told him all he knew of the treasures of the
country. With his help the Englishmen went among the
neighbouring tribes, and so noble a memory did Ralegh
leave behind him that long afterward he was still spoken
of to chance travellers. They saw gold in various places
and took with them many specimens, but they never seem
to have found it in any extraordinary quantity. One
incident is worth recording for the great influence which
it exercised over the leader's mind in days when his
thoughts turned wearily to those lands. He heard from

his lieutenant, Keymis, that as he was being led by a shorter road to join the others, his Indian guide at a certain place wished to lead him aside. Supposing it to be some natural beauty or other Keymis refused and continued in his path. In after years that wayside halting-place was the point on which rested the destinies of both master and man.

In all these inquiries there is something more than a mere search for gold. Ralegh looked to this only as a means to an end, the proof with which he was to persuade the English nation of the value of the land for colonizing or conquest. 'I could indeed have returned a good quantity of gold ready cast, if I had not shot at another mark than present profit[1].' We find him holding grave discourse with Topiawari on the best means of penetrating to the interior. In his dealings with the natives, in his insistence upon payment for all commodities received, and generally in his orderly and moderate counsels, we discern far more of the colonizer than the treasure-hunter. Moreover, even in those strange latitudes, his mind was full of his Virginian colony, and it was part of his intention, but for the severity of the weather, to go thither 'for the relief,' as he tells us, 'of those English I have planted there.'

The actual results effected in the expedition may seem small when compared with the expenditure of time, money, and energy; but they were none the less real. A path had been formed for some considerable way into the interior, the presence of gold had been ascertained, the rich and productive nature of the land was known, and many of the native tribes had been won to the English interest. The return to England was full of hardships, but otherwise unimportant, and in the August of 1595 they sighted the the shores of Devon. There is no doubt that Ralegh was bitterly disappointed with the reception he met with. He

---

[1] *Discoverie of Guiana*, p. 60.

returned with what he considered sufficient proof of success, and renewed enthusiasm for the cause of Guianian
exploration. He found the Queen still cold and irre-
sponsive, his enemies ready with malicious suggestions,
and even his best friends looking askance at the small
issue of great expectations. His wondrous stories were
currently looked upon as fabrications, and a slander was
circulated that he had never been further from home than
Cornwall. Even such results as were undeniable had their
value lessened by the insinuations of envy. To defend
himself, and further his schemes, Ralegh published his
famous *Discoverie of Guiana*, in which he answered his
enemies calumnies, and told in glowing words the wonders
of that new land oversea. No one of his works has the
same fresh interest as this. It sprang at once into
popularity, and amused and delighted thousands whom no
arguments could convince. But nothing could alter the
unfavourable view taken even by the best men in that day
of Ralegh's aims and character. The variety of his pur-
suits made him cross the purposes of many, and brilliance
has always a foe in mediocrity. Nor is it worth while to
give a thought to the accusation of indiscriminate falsehood,
which was current at the time, and was revived in after days
by Hume. The mind of the man was already open to
marvels, and the evidence on which he related his details
was in his eyes perfectly unimpeachable—the testimony
of such natives as Topiawari, whom he had no reason to
distrust, as well as the accounts of so highly civilized
a nation as Spain.

Many causes kept Ralegh at home, but his mind was
still on his ventures. In the February of 1596, Keymis
was dispatched on a mission similar to the last, but with
inefficient forces and under widely different conditions.
He found that the Spanish reinforcements expected by
De Berreo had come, and that some of the routes were

blocked. With some difficulty he made his way to the mouth of the Coroni, and found that Topiawari was dead and the English connexion broken. But one thing he discovered of unique importance—he found that the path among the hills, where the Indian guide had wished him to turn aside, led to a gold-mine of great richness. But he had too small a force to attempt to reach it, so with the news he returned to England.

Towards the end of the same year Ralegh dispatched a single ship on the same errand, under the command of a Captain Leonard Berry, but the vessel returned without having effected anything of value [1]. In all the years of active anxious life which succeeded he never lost sight of his plans, and strove as best he might to keep up his connexion with old acquaintances. We have not yet complete knowledge of all the forces which detained him at home. Untoward events which affected his own safety happened; the men in power, the Queen herself, were always somewhat' sceptical and wholly uneager; and he lacked the private wealth necessary to make any attempt a lasting success. We know that at one time Burghley gave him £50 for a new voyage, and Sir Robert Cecil ventured a ship of which the hull alone was valued at £800. But it has been argued, with considerable probability, that the Cecils aided Ralegh in his plans merely to be quit of his presence at home, and opposed him whenever they found that he intended to send another. But we know that then and ever after it was Ralegh's opinion that, by such neglect, a great opportunity had been passed over for extending and enriching his land, and giving new scope to the energies of his people.

[1] *Hakluyt*, xiii. 692.

c

VIII.

We have seen that Ralegh on his return was immersed in public business, and was unable to continue his Guiana enterprises on account of the many demands on his labour. The source of it all was the Cadiz expedition, which we may regard as his most successful naval or military achievement, though he shares with other men the honour of the victory. Originally a plan of Sir John Hawkins', it was revived in 1596 by the Lord Admiral Howard as the most effective means of striking a blow at the Spanish power. Essex was joined with him in the supreme command, and Ralegh (whose value was known, though he was still in disfavour at Court) and Lord Thomas Howard were added as councillors. The plans of the enterprise were varied from day to day till the leaders were well-nigh distracted. It is probable that the original commission was directed more to the destruction of the Spanish navy than to the acquirement of spoil by the sack of a rich city. The former interpretation of the mandate was stoutly upheld by Ralegh as the more statesmanlike, but subsequent events showed that no blow more crushing than the taking of Cadiz could have been levelled at the strength and pride of Spain. Ralegh was delayed in joining the others owing to the extreme difficulty he found in making his levies [1]—a delay which his enemies did not fail to turn to malicious account [2].

The English fleet consisted of seventeen Queen's ships and seventy-six hired transport vessels, and was divided into four squadrons. A Dutch squadron of some twenty-four ships was also present, but took little part in the actual battle. It is hard to arrive at an exact estimate of

---

[1] Ralegh to Cecil. *Cecil Papers*, vol. xl. § 60, cited in Edwards' *Ralegh*, ii. p. 129.

[2] Archbishop Tenison, *Baconiana*, DCLVII. 8.

the Spanish strength which blocked the bay of Cadiz, but there seem to have been present nearly sixty tall vessels, with from eight to twenty galleys attending. On the way Ralegh's squadron was directed to sail well out to sea, and take up a position at the mouth of Cadiz harbour to prevent the escape of any of the enemy's ships. This almost led to a disaster, for in an over-confident temper Essex and Howard determined to make a raid on the town before attacking the fleet. Fortunately for the success of the venture, Ralegh returned in the nick of time, and by argument and expostulation succeeded in turning the admirals from such ruinous policy[1]. Every preparation was made for immediate battle. Ralegh from his vessel cried out to Essex 'Intramus,' and the perfervid earl in his excitement flung his plumed cap into the sea.

The arrangements for the fight were made with difficulty. Ralegh wrote hurriedly to the Lord Admiral, and by ten o'clock at night it was settled that he should lead the van, while the others advanced with the body of the fleet. The first dawn saw the opening of the fight. Ralegh in the *Warspight* made straight for the greater galleons. Then ensued the tempest of attack and repulse, shot and fire and carnage, which mark a decisive naval engagement. He had many old scores to avenge on Spain, and the death of Sir Richard Grenville was still fresh in his memory. He had orders not to board till the promised fly-boats were sent to his aid, but as none came he set out to meet Essex in a skiff, and cried that, orders or none, he would board at once. 'I will second you on my soul,' the admiral said, and the *Warspight* with generous rivalry was forced once more to the front of the battle. The

---

[1] This is the account given in his own narrative ; but his share may easily be exaggerated, and is flatly contradicted by Sir William Monson, the captain of Essex' ship. ('Naval Tracts' in Churchill's *Voyages*, 1704, iii. 185.)

Spaniards grounded, and the issue of the day was clear. Then came the attendant horrors of massacre and rapine ; 'if any man had a desire to see Hell itself, it was there most livelily figured [1].'

In the sea-fight Ralegh was so terribly wounded that he could take little share in the land-attack, but from his litter he saw enough to bear testimony to the wisdom and valour of Essex. He returned home in August with an authentic account of the engagement, and was able to set at rest the perplexed mind of the Council.

The result of the great English victory was the paralysis of the Spanish nation, a shock from which her recovery was slow. Ralegh's anti-Spanish policy had received abundant realization. But the immediate consequence at home was a succession of wretched squabbles on the division of the Cadiz spoils. The men who had led the battle, the Essexes and Raleghs, were content with meagre portions, but the under-officers lined their purses well ere ever the sum was estimated. The Queen was naturally angry, but she showed it by copying the same fault on a more regal scale. She haggled and cheated with the avarice of one half-ashamed of the part, and the treasury was augmented, while the poor captains went penniless.

But for Ralegh the expedition, if it brought little gain, was fruitful of one important consequence. The affair at Cadiz had brought together Essex and his rival, and in the common joy of success something of the old jealousy was forgotten. It was through this late-resumed friendship that Ralegh's return to Court was effected, though the suit of Essex was not made with the best of graces and was rather passive permission than active help. In May 1597 he had an interview with the Queen and resumed his duties as Captain of the Guard. Once more his old favour seemed to be returning, and we find him united with Essex and

[1] *Relation of Cadiz Action*, p. 72.

Cecil in a sort of diplomatic triumvirate. This was the beginning of that close connexion with Essex' fortunes which lowered Sir Walter so greatly in the popular esteem, and became the fount of most of the calumnies with which his name has been associated. The character of one at least of the trio is not hard to read. Essex is the current type of high instincts and a generous heart joined to a singularly passionate and unthinking nature. His powers of mind were considerable, his honour was never seriously questioned; but by an accident of fate he was placed in that very position in all the world for which nature had least fitted him. He was baited by Elizabeth from private caprice; his sudden rise and the brilliance of his fame brought round him a crowd of enemies; and his friends were either of his own stamp or foes in disguise who urged him to his ruin by fostering his natural impulses.. The position craved wary walking, and the earl was scarcely the man to see it. He did not recognize the insecure basis on which his power rested; he never quite realized that by the Queen he stood or fell, nor followed Bacon's quaintly-quoted advice against his arrogance, 'Martha, Martha, attendis ad plurima; unum sufficit[1].' The tragic issue was always at hand, and it is with something of dramatic irony that he goes the precipitate path to his fall. His relation to Cecil is hard to understand on the insufficient information which we possess. The two were diametrically opposed in nature, and could not long work in the same harness. We shall have occasion to discuss more fully the question of Cecil's character in connexion with his subsequent dealings with Ralegh, but for the present it seems undeniable that he had a hand in inciting the unhappy earl to rush head-long to his doom. With Ralegh, on the other hand, the relations of Essex seem tolerably clear. Both had a great capacity for enthusiasm, both were in love with swift, brilliant

---

[1] Bacon, *Works*, xi. pp. 179–185.

action, and intolerant of the common. We have seen that their early dislike sprang from opposing interests. We shall see that the renewed ill-feeling which lasted to the end owed its origin to this fatal kinship in temper.

But the new connexion seemed to begin in perfect amity. Wild rumours came from abroad of a new Armada, mustering to revenge Cadiz. Ralegh, in his *Opinion upon the Spanish Alarum*, declared that the best way of frustrating any Spanish attack was to strike beforehand at some portion of her power. A new expedition was determined upon with Ralegh and Essex in joint command; and on July 10, 1597, the fleet sailed from Plymouth Sound. At first nothing but misfortune was its fate—the death of men and the loss of ships. We find that Essex took the untoward result sorely to heart, and Ralegh in a sudden kindness wrote to Cecil asking some 'comfort from her Majesty to the Lord General, who is dismayed by these mischances even to death, although there could not be more done by any man upon the earth[1].' Once more, on August 17, after many expenses which fell solely on Essex, the fleet set sail. There is little need to enter into the details of the voyage. Ralegh separated himself from the rest, and on his meeting with Essex at Flores learned that his absence had been the ground of an attempt by busybodies to stir up a quarrel between the two commanders. Once more they separated, and on Ralegh's arrival at Fayal he waited three days on the rest. On the fourth he lost patience, attacked, and took the town with his single squadron.

We cannot choose but exempt him from all blame in the matter. The moment needed action; to wait was not to risk but to ruin all, and give the fame of the achievement, if it actually took place, to some other than the English fleet. But none the less did he commit a breach of military discipline, and we can understand the anger of Essex when

[1] *Domestic Correspondence: Elizabeth*, ccv. § 177.

he heard the tale. He wisely refused to punish the offender, but he let the thing rankle in his heart, and the Meyrickes and Blounts of his party kept the offence from falling into the background. All ostensible quarrel was healed by the intervention of Lord Thomas Howard, but the earl's wounded pride and disappointment, as well as the clamouring of his retainers, first gave rise to the open and recognized hostility which began to exist between himself and Ralegh. In October the fleet came home with considerable plunder, and the Queen was satisfied for the moment. Ralegh's reputation among men of affairs was notably increased, and we find the Council commending to his care the south coast naval defences.

But from the moment of his return the predominant interest of his mind was less warlike enterprise than the dangerous game of courtiership. But for the mischief-makers on both sides, it is probable that the rivalry with Essex would have been conducted with respect and some degree of friendship. As it was, he did him one friendly service, for in persuading the Queen to make him Earl Marshal he settled the vexed question of precedence between Essex and the Lord High Admiral.

The special circumstances of the time, and the imminency of a war with Spain, had brought about a strange conjunction between Cecil, Essex, and Ralegh. Of the three Cecil went his solitary path unmoved by the hopes and visions of his coadjutors. It is reasonable to suppose that the union gave Ralegh a knowledge of his rival's character, an insight into his aims and desires, which coloured his subsequent conduct towards him. The countenance which he gave to the Southampton marriage, and his strange outburst of contempt in the Queen's presence, had already placed the earl's fortunes on a tottering base. Then came the offer and acceptance of the Irish governorship, and the long catalogue of catastrophes which throng the last years

of his life.   It is hard to decide whether Essex' Irish policy
was indeed in advance of his time and proceeded from
statesmanlike foresight, or whether it was but the easy
toleration of the man.   At any rate he could not escape
opposition from Ralegh, the administrator who had begun
his career with the strictest coercion.   The man who sought
the conciliation rather than the conquest of rebels could
not have much in common with the man who had been
unscrupulous in the cause of annihilation.   There is little
need to wonder if opposition in policy became the parent
of distrust and fear.

On Ralegh's part, in the last scene of the tragedy there
seems no reason for indecision.   The reports of the intended
murder of Essex and Ralegh at the hands of one another
may be set down to the excitement of followers.   Blount's
confession on the scaffold is the coping-stone on our pile of
counter-evidence.   But the famous letter[1] to Cecil is posi-
tive proof that Ralegh's feelings in the matter were full of
bitterness.   The question of life and death was not then
before the Council ; the matter was simply whether pardon
should be granted or such incapacities laid on the prisoner
as would render him powerless to meddle with the affairs of
England.   Of all Ralegh's correspondence this letter is least
admirable.   It is full of malicious worldly wisdom and
a perfectly gratuitous unfairness to the unhappy earl.
There is no need to censure the writer for the lack of
virtues which he never laid claim to, but we are driven
to confess that such language was an ungracious return for
past unkindness.   More it is needless to say, and it is pure
folly to assume Ralegh's partnership in the more bitter
extravagance of the sentence of death.   But it was clearly
stamped upon the popular mind that in the whole matter
he had played a part which, if not actually base, was wholly
unworthy ; and at the last hour of his life he thought fit to

[1] Edwards' *Ralegh*, vol. ii. (Letters) pp. 222, 223.

clear himself of some part of the blame which men had cast
upon him.   He had been accused of mocking Essex in his
last moments, and blowing tobacco smoke at him.   Nay,
rather, he said, ' I take God to witness that I shed tears for
him when he died.   I confess I was of a contrary faction.
But I knew that my Lord of Essex was a noble gentleman,
and that it would be worse with me when he was gone.
For those that set up against him did afterwards set themselves against me.'   The confession is ample for our purpose.
Towards Essex he felt an admiration mingled with affection,
and a jealousy not without malice.

IX.

The death of Essex marked the acme of Ralegh's Court
favour ; thereafter came doubtful years and the crash of
a new *régime*.   It is worth while to halt for one moment
and consider the way in which his contemporaries regarded
him, his rivals in office as well as the mass of the people.
He had fought his way to a great position in the realm, and
it is a curious question how men looked upon the steps of
his upward course.   His fame with posterity has been so
great that we are apt to think of him as the admired of all,
the seer and enthusiast who led a delighted nation in the
paths of wisdom.

It comes with something of a shock to most to find out
how little this opinion is true.   It is possible to find men
who have had smaller circles of friends, but it is hard to
find one with a larger crowd of virulent foes.   He was
hated by all and sundry, from the citizens of London to
the courtiers who jostled him in the Queen's antechamber.
And the reason of it is not hard to seek, if we look shrewdly
at his life.

He was above all things a man of action, and as such
was loved by his soldiers and sailors, and the folk of Devon

and the West who shared in his spirit. But the men who found themselves outstripped in the Queen's favour by one who owed his success to audacity and uncommon cleverness may be pardoned if they felt little love for the intruder. The ruck of Court followers were too heartily despised by the busy man of affairs to be kindly affectioned towards him. Nor did he succeed better with the grave councillors. With the swift intuition of genius he saw things far off, and with the arrogance of genius he laughed at the slow plodders who were toiling at their routine tasks. Moreover, he was a firebrand in any council-chamber. The Queen's policy in her later years was all for peace, and her statesmen took the colour of her views ; but this man hankered always for battle and enterprise, and laughed at vain measures of conciliation. Nor must we forget that this chivalrous gentleman of subsequent history did not always preserve either his chivalry or his gentility. We have abundant evidence of the extraordinary charm of Ralegh's intercourse with his friends, the 'exceeding good parts of nature in him'[1]; but it seems equally clear that he could show abundant discourtesy to an enemy. In his dealings with ordinary men he was frequently insolent, rash, and capricious, and such unadvised conduct was soon to rebound to his own disgrace.

Of his place in the mind of the people we can form a similar estimate. He had risen by Court favour to great ostensible wealth and power, and his success had been redeemed by no such lavish popular outlays as had gilded the careers of others. To the ordinary man he must have seemed one who had risen by unscrupulous means and had kept his place by an unequally unsparing avarice. Again, his great deeds in the Indies and the Spanish wars would scarcely be put to his credit, when his motive was always believed to be self-aggrandisement. His very popularity

[1] Northumberland's *Correspondence*, cited by Gardiner, i. p. 59.

with his followers would militate against him, for the crafts-
man and the trader look with suspicion on the man who is
a lord among paid servants.   Rumours of his unscrupulousness and ambition, as well as the extraordinary charge of
atheism, would filter down from their betters; and their
feelings towards him would have all the bitterness of the
virtuous and dull against wicked talent.   His currently-
reported part in the death of the popular favourite Essex
would not help his reputation.   Finally, he would be injured
by the attitude he assumed towards the people and popular
claims.   He had always a contempt for the homage of the
crowd, and would never go one step from his path to seek
it.   With the spirit of a grandee he scorned the rabble, and
never deferred to its opinion.   Like Bacon, he might have
said, 'I do not love the word *people.*' We believe him to
have been liberal in the truest sense, to have loved the
freedom of the English race as his own life, and come
forward as the champion of what was just and reasonable in
popular demands.   But he had no rhetorical artifices to
win applause, and his genuine services met with scant
recognition.

Of his true attitude to the people and their interests we
can learn in the incidents of his Parliamentary life.   He sat
in the House of Commons from 1585 to 1602, first for
Devon and then for Cornwall, and took considerable part
in the conduct of business.   In this sphere, as in every
other in which he laboured, he laboured hard and well.
We find him taking part in the thankless toil of committee-
making, and becoming something of an authority on the
minutiae of Parliamentary procedure.   In 1593, and again
in 1601, he spoke at length on the Spanish question,
sketched the extent and importance of the power of Spain
and its probable conduct if unchecked, and offered valuable
advice on the manner in which the subsidies should be
levied.   He answered Cecil's sentimental plea for a uniform

payment by showing the extreme injustice of the poor paying the same as the rich, an injustice not alleviated by extreme necessity. On the question of the incidence of taxation, Ralegh took the popular side at a time when little credit was attached to the advocacy of a reformed financial policy. On the question of religious toleration he spoke with a certain voice. He opposed the measures against the Brownists, and in his words there is one sentence which is admirable as a concise statement of a great political maxim. 'The law is hard which taketh life, or sendeth into banishment, where men's intentions shall be judged by a jury; and they shall be judges what another man meant[1].' On one other question we have some record of his views. He was utterly opposed to statutes like the Statute of Tillage, which laid restrictions and commandments on the farmer. 'For my part,' said he, 'I do not like the constraining of men to use their ground at our wills.' The current *Labourage et Pâturage* maxim, which the statesmen of his day borrowed from France, had little power over his mind. On the contrary, he advocated the entire freedom of trade. 'I think the best course is to set corn at liberty, and leave every man free; which is the desire of a true Englishman.'

It is impossible to attribute such words and actions to a definite political policy. The man's mind was too busy in other spheres to be able to afford the concentration and the labour necessary for a great statesman. His politics were the outcome of his natural love of fairness and liberty, and partly of his power of shrewd perception and accurate generalization. But in matters which closely affected his own or his friends' interests he was swayed by less statesmanlike considerations. He defended the grants of patents on Cornish tin as the only means of keeping the metal at a proper value and giving the workmen fair wages for their

[1] D'Ewes, *Journal of the Parliament of Queen Elizabeth*, p. 76.

labour. It is not the people of England whom he is thinking of now. It is the people of Cornwall, the men of his own countryside, whose interests had always lain nearest to his heart. And indeed we cannot blame him for it ; his thoughts were always concrete and local ; and even when he attempts to consider general results, he is swayed by personal feelings and a thousand memories.

But in spite of this we may assert that Ralegh's Parliamentary policy was liberal and popular beyond any statesman's of the time. And yet it in no way served to alter the common verdict. The proceedings of Parliament were too little known to have much interest for the ordinary citizen, and to him and his class Ralegh remained the ambitious courtier, the able and unscrupulous soldier, and the man who wrought ever for his own ends.

X.

The history of Ralegh's life is now complicated by a thousand difficulties and entangled in the maze of doubt which shrouds the death of Elizabeth and the first months of James' reign. As the hours of the Queen drew to their close, the minds of her councillors were perplexed by many plots and petty diplomacies. To the popular mind the accession of James seemed indisputable, but to the Court the question was still open. It has been estimated that some fourteen claimants aspired to the crown of England, and of these three at least were considerable enough to give grave anxiety. The more extreme Catholics upheld the claims of the Spanish Infanta as tracing her descent direct from the Plantagenets. But such a far-away genealogy could have little attraction for a nation never given to antiquarian research. The Parliamentary title, again, lay with the family of Suffolk, since, by the will of Henry VIII, the House of Stuart had been excluded from the throne, which was to pass to the children of his niece, Lady Frances. The death of the Queen of Scots deprived this claim of the argument of necessity, and the Parliament were willing enough to recognize the Stuart title. But even here arose a difficulty, for by a curious legal quibble James' claim seemed less valid than that of his cousin Arabella Stuart, inasmuch as by English law no alien could inherit land in England. Yet it was patent to all that a ruling monarch with power to make good his title was the only possible successor, and to James the eyes of the nation turned. It was impossible to negotiate with him as heir-apparent, since Elizabeth to the last refused to nominate her successor; and, in consequence, the history of the last months of her life is a history of networks of plot and intrigue carried on by her ministers with the Court of Scotland.

The two men who figured most prominently in these negotiations were Lord Henry Howard, a younger son of the Earl of Surrey, and Cecil himself. As for the first, of all the evil characters of the time there is none whose villainy is better authenticated. A man of considerable learning and native shrewdness, he early saw the direction in which his interests lay, and began a correspondence with James, which for gross adulation and mendacity stands by itself in the annals of intrigue. In consequence, James looked to him as one of the warmest supporters of his claim, and set him apart for special honour in the event of his success. But Cecil was not long behind, and, taking advantage of Lord Mar's embassy to London, he entered into communications with the King of Scots. James saw clearly the importance of this new help, and availed himself of it gladly. It is certain that at first the name of Cecil, as the foe of Essex and the sworn confidant of Elizabeth, was particularly obnoxious to him; but James had the rare merit of recognizing the possibility of conversion in others, and though he never entertained a great affection for his new adviser, he gave him his full confidence and raised him to the summit of power.

In such a condition of affairs the position of Ralegh was that of an alien. He had no claims to friendship with Howard, and to Cecil he was never more than a respected rival. He saw in the approaching end of Elizabeth the death of many of his brightest hopes. Already he knew something of the character of the King of Scots, and he could not hope that James would lend a ready ear to his great schemes of colonization or anti-Spanish enterprise. Further, he was a holder of many well-paid offices, and he could not expect to continue to enjoy them. There is evidence that he sought an alliance with Cecil, but the minister was deaf to his plans, and in something like despair he turned to the only man of rank with whom he had any influence, and allowed his name to be coupled with that of Lord Cobham.

Meanwhile, in the busy correspondence with Scotland, his reputation was being shadowed and calumniated. There is no evidence that Cecil in his letters had any more sinister intention than to remove an opponent from power whom he considered dangerous to the national welfare. In all the relations of the two an honourable rivalry was maintained, and Ralegh at all times upheld the uprightness of Cecil's conduct while he censured its unkindness. But with Howard the case was different. There is the clearest proof [1] that he purposed by fair means or foul to implicate Ralegh in a treasonable plot, that his ruin might be secured. The result was not quite equal to his expectations; but one thing at least he achieved, that James came to the south with a mind filled with the profoundest distrust of Ralegh and his friends.

[1] See especially 'Howard to Lord Mar,' p. 44 sqq., and 'Howard to Cecil, contra Ralegh and Cobham,' printed in the Appendix to Edwards' *Ralegh*, vol. ii.

Then came the wretched story of his meeting with the King at Burghley, and his subsequent loss of his Captaincy of the Guard. He was compensated for it by the remission of a payment of £300, chargeable upon his governorship of Jersey. He saw his fate clearly from the beginning. The loss of one of his offices was merely the prelude to a general disgrace. For one brief moment the baser parts of his nature got the pre-eminence. It was clear that Cecil and Howard had influenced the King in his decision, but it was no less clear that the former had acted from sufficiently honourable motives. But Ralegh was crazed with anxiety and disappointment, and forthwith wrote a letter to James, accusing Cecil of the chief part in Essex' death, a piece of malice as unwise as it was ineffectual.

The immediate result of these misfortunes was to ally Ralegh more closely with Cobham. Meanwhile, the air was charged with plots and rumours of plots. A small body of malcontent Catholics, consisting of a mad priest named Watson, Sir Gervase Markham, and George Brooke, a brother of Cobham, entered into a conspiracy to wring from the King a universal toleration. Following a bad Scots precedent, they resolved to kidnap James, and keep him in their hands till he granted their petition. Lord Grey, who, Puritan as he was, had at first joined their ranks, withdrew as soon as the preposterous nature of the scheme was apparent. The affair was doomed from the first; the leaders only half believed in it; and when it finally broke up on the rumour that the Government had news of it, the conspirators were taken with the greatest ease.

About the same time the Count d'Arenbergh had come over as an ambassador on behalf of the Archduke Albert, the governor of the Spanish Low Countries, to negotiate for a peace between England and Spain. For some reason or other, Cobham was brought into close connexion with this Spanish envoy, and was made the recipient of an offer of money to try and further the peace proposal. Fragments of plots had been drifting in his vain and empty mind, and now he seemed to see a way to their realization. His first dealings with the foreign ambassador were perfectly open, but soon we find him engaged on more doubtful business. He had a vague design of placing Arabella Stuart on the throne, and at the same time he proposed that a sum of six hundred thousand crowns should be placed at his disposal to carry on his work. He asked his brother, George Brooke, to join him, but he refused, being already busied with all the conspiracy he desired.

It is an ascertained fact that Cobham now turned his attention to Ralegh, and sought to make him a participant of his schemes. On at least two occasions he offered him money, and it is probable that he communicated most of his plans. Of Ralegh's conduct, though every detail has been discussed for three hundred years, we can only guess. At this time he was in a state of great despondency and bitterness. He had been compelled to resign his dearest office, the Wardenship of the Stannaries, and his wine licences seemed on the verge of recall. The matter of Durham House had given him acute annoyance, and on all sides he saw his enemies triumphant, and his aims frustrated. It is not to be wondered at if he listened to Cobham's wild talk with a sort of capricious enjoyment. Mr. Gardiner's admirable conjecture seems the truest explanation of this difficult point, and this, or something like this, seems to have been the order of events. The fact that Brooke was engaged in Watson's treason made Cecil suspect that his brother could not be guiltless. Consequently he summoned Ralegh before the Council and cross-questioned him on his friend's conduct. Ralegh, with his mind full of dark sayings and vague hints which he had always looked on with contempt, spoke what he believed to be the plain truth, and declared that he knew nothing of Cobham's actions. Then he reflected afterwards that Cobham was none the less guilty of treason, and that, if he wished to be free, it was his duty to tell what he knew. With some disgust at the thankless task, he wrote to Cecil telling him that he believed Cobham to be engaged in a plot with d'Arenbergh to set the Lady Arabella on the throne. Cobham was arrested, whether on this letter or on his brother's confession we cannot tell, and lodged in the Tower. Then Ralegh began to realize the full danger of his position, and remembered how he had often talked wildly in Cobham's presence of his grievances against the Government. He sent Keymis with a letter to the prisoner, bidding him hold his tongue and remember that the only witness against him was his brother, and one witness was not sufficient for a condemnation. But meantime, Cobham had seen Ralegh's first letter to Cecil; he was naturally enraged, and, showing the letter to the Council, denounced Ralegh as a traitor and conspirator.

To the mind of the Council the affair looked more than suspicious. Ralegh was arrested on July 17, and sent to join the other conspirators in the Tower. This was the finishing touch to his misery. His body was worn with toils, and his mind had long been harassed with a thousand cares. Above all, the fate of his wife and family was ever before him. For their sake he must end this wretched farce, and in a fortnight so low had he sunk in health and spirits that he attempted suicide, after writing a touching farewell to Lady Ralegh. Happily he failed in his purpose, and was left to bide the brunt of his trial.

Of the trial it is possible to write only with the greatest caution. The main incidents and the result are perfectly clear, but the exact amount of evidence on each side, and the impression produced by such evidence on the jurors, remain and must remain in the deepest obscurity. Four matters must be considered by any one who would examine the case—the exact nature of the accusation and the proof brought forward to support it, the prisoner's defence, the justice of the whole proceedings tried by modern notions of equity, and their legality tried by the existing law of England.

The accusation as stated by Coke was that of complicity in a plot in some way connected with Watson's treason, with the object of setting Arabella on the throne by the help of a Spanish army, in return for which the supremacy of the Spanish over the English power was to be established. An accurate account was given of Ralegh's negotiations with Cobham at a supper-party, depending for its truth solely on the fact that the two were known friends, and that such a thing might possibly have happened. He was further accused of connivance at an attempt of Cobham's to antedate a letter, apparently on no ground whatever. He was accused of having listened to or accepted an offer of a bribe from d'Arenbergh, and as proof Keymis' confession was produced, in which he told of an interview between Ralegh and Cobham at a time when the latter was in communication with the Spanish envoy.

The evidence brought forward was of three kinds—unauthenticated rumours, depositions and examinations of various prisoners, and the avowed conduct of the accused. The members of Watson's plot had always held, it seemed, that Ralegh and Cobham were really of their number. This evidence pointed more particularly to Cobham, but it was held to refer to Ralegh on the ground of close friendship. Watson in especial had made the direct statement that he had always heard from Brooke that both Ralegh and Cobham were strongly inclined to the Spanish interest. Again, there remained the confession of Cobham, in which he clearly implicated Ralegh; the deposition of Keymis, who swore to meetings between the two; Ralegh's own confession of the offer of money made to him; and the evidence of a sailor who had heard talk on the quay at Lisbon of Ralegh's friendliness to Spanish claims. In the third class there was the known disaffection of Ralegh consequent on the loss of place and money, sundry unwise words spoken in the ears of untrustworthy friends, and his singularly suspicious letter to Cobham in which he had advised him to secrecy.

Little, if any, of such evidence is important or relevant according to our ideas, but it seemed otherwise to his judges. It was necessary for Ralegh to prove that there was no reason why he should have any part in such a conspiracy as Cobham's, that any proof of a particular act of complicity was false, and that those actions of his which seemed open to suspicion could be simply explained.

The trial took place at Winchester on the seventeenth of November and the days following. Coke, as Attorney-General, conducted the prosecution with a barbarity and confusion remarkable even in one who considered that a blunt honesty and a phenomenal acquaintance with the law of England counterbalanced the entire absence of all other virtues. To his harshness Ralegh replied with modesty and good temper, and we have it on record that the feelings of the spectators, at first violently hostile, were converted by his demeanour into friendliness. His defence he conducted alone, and with no little skill and good sense. The argument on the inherent probability of his being engaged in such a plot he answered well by pointing to his past record. Was it likely, he asked, that he who had all his life been the bitterest foe of Spain should now be found conspiring in her interest? Was it likely that he who knew the character of Arabella should seek to set her on the throne at a time when all was prosperous at home and abroad, and a lawful successor was present in the reigning king? Was it likely, too, that he would make a confidant of a man like Cobham?

The second, and more formidable, proof from Cobham's depositions he met in two ways. He utterly denied the truth of the evidence, and argued reasonably enough that Cobham had contradicted himself so frequently that his word was of no value. Then he demanded to be brought face to face with his accuser. This request was supported by Cecil, but the judges without exception declared it unjustified by law. They saw too well what would be the result of such a meeting, how the unhappy Cobham would still further confuse his statements and make a conviction on his evidence seem palpably absurd. Finding at last that the Court intended to abide by the particular confession of Cobham's which accused his friend, Ralegh tried a new line, and questioned the legality of the course which the prosecution was taking. Two statutes of Edward VI, confirmed by a subsequent statute of Philip and Mary, had declared that no man could be convicted of treason except by two witnesses[1]. But Popham replied with the quibble, which was nevertheless universally accepted at the time, that the second statute limited the action of the first to certain specified treasons and abolished it in regard to others.

The third proof, based on his avowed offer from Cobham, and the highly suspicious letter he had sent by Keymis, Ralegh found the hardest to deal with. He could only say that Cobham's offer had been made before d'Arenbergh's arrival in England, and that such money was intended to assist only in the furtherance of the negotiations. In the matter of the letter he foolishly denied the whole business, and as Keymis' veracity was perfectly well known this action did considerable harm to his own cause. To

[1] 1 Ed. VI. cap. 12, and 6 Ed. VI. cap. 11; 1 and 2 Phil. and Mary, cap. 10.

the minds of his judges it was clear that at least he was not wholly truthful.

The proofs from the *à priori* possibility and from the various depositions had not been substantiated, but two things had been made evident,—that an offer of money had been made, and that throughout the trial he had not spoken all he knew. Consequently the question, as Serjeant Phelps declared, lay between the truthfulness of Cobham and Ralegh. Cobham had been proved utterly false, and Ralegh had not shown himself free from the same fault. If we grant the assumptions made in any treason trial, that one witness could bring about a verdict of guilty, and that the mere listening to treasonable proposals constituted a treasonable offence, we can understand the feelings in the minds of the jury. After an absence of fifteen minutes they returned a verdict of guilty, and Popham pronounced sentence of death.

To us the whole affair has an element of the fantastic and absurd. The proof was flimsy in the extreme. It is probable that Cobham in his folly had made half-plans for some plot or other, and the French ambassador Beaumont's dispatch[1] to his master seems to give certainty to the supposition; but no reliable evidence on the matter has been brought forward. As to Ralegh's connexion with Cobham we have already considered its possible extent. That he committed a fault which at any time could be construed into treason is doubtful at the best; but it is perfectly certain that the Court were in possession of no proof of such treason. The whole conduct of the case, the private examinations, the refusal to bring the accuser and accused face to face, are repugnant to our ideas of justice. The one thing proved, that Ralegh had received an offer of money before d'Arenbergh's arrival and

[1] *Beaumont to the King of France*, from the King's MSS., quoted in a note to Gardiner, vol. i. p. 103.

immediately refused it, was in no way treason; and if Ralegh had shown himself to have dabbled in falsehood, we should consider that Cobham's evidence fell utterly to the ground from its frequent contradictions. There could be no question between the veracity of a man who was driven by hard straits into a trivial prevarication and one whose contempt of the truth came near to insanity. Looking back from the vantage-ground of years we see clearly that Ralegh was wholly guiltless of the charge and that his condemnation was a miracle of injustice.

On the other hand we must acquit his judges of any wilful false practice. Judging him by the letter of the law of treason as it then stood, and taking into consideration the light in which treason was regarded, we acknowledge that his condemnation was not illegal. Treason was regarded as so terrible an offence, not only against the king but against the peace of the nation and the prosperity of private citizens, that for an acquittal it was necessary not that a man should not be proved guilty, but that he should clearly establish his entire innocence. Cross-examination of a witness was not permitted that there might be no chance for a bold criminal to overawe a more timid accuser. Again, it was regarded as established by law that one witness was sufficient to secure a conviction. In such circumstances it was a judge's duty to consider Cobham's deposition true in spite of his known character, if the conduct of Ralegh could not be proved entirely free from falsehood. The fact of Cobham's repeated disavowals they might set down to terror or the old kindness for a friend.

We know now that Ralegh's character was honourable and truthful beyond his time, but to his contemporaries it appeared far otherwise. His narrative of Guiana enterprise had not improved the reputation for veracity of one who was always looked upon as unscrupulous. In the course of his trial he had made one wholly false statement, and in various matters had not spoken the complete truth. This was sufficient and more than sufficient for his judges. Their action, always within the letter of the law, was justified by popular feeling and past experience.

The sentence of death was never executed. Ralegh, Cobham, and Grey, as they stood on the scaffold at Winchester, received a reprieve from the King. It seems unlikely that James ever intended that they should die, and in any case the entreaties of the foreign ambassadors and the intercession of friends had altered his mind. Ralegh himself, both through his wife and various letters to the Lords of Council, begged for life with an urgency of which he was afterwards ashamed. But James had a desire to hear the last confessions of his prisoners, and he wished to deliver the pardons with some dramatic effect. So the scaffolds were prepared, the dying testimonies written and delivered, before the gracious monarch interfered. With this pathetic piece of mock-heroic Ralegh passed from the stage of active life to the enforced quiet of the Tower.

In all these calamitous changes it is possible to see the effect of Ralegh's previous deeds and native qualities. He had ever been haughty and rash of tongue, and a crowd of enemies sprang up around him in the day of misfortune. He had sought wealth and added place to place with the result that he loomed in the popular mind as a self-seeking adventurer, and when a great crisis had come the loss of his honours inclined him to turbulent despair. Above all, he had used his great gifts in that domain for which he was least suited ; the glamour of Court display was always about him ; and it was not till late in the day, when the grey walls of a prison sobered his fancy, that he turned his mind to work worthy of his powers.

XI.

For fourteen years the Tower claimed its prisoner, and
in the history of his life we are removed from the world
of deeds to the inner life of study and speculation. His
position was thick with gratuitous hardships; he had bare
quarters, and such little liberty as he at first enjoyed was
soon restricted by the malice of enemies. From the year
1606 onward we know that his health declined [1], and his
mind was tormented with the misfortunes of his family and
the blank wall which seemed to have stopped his once
hopeful career. But it is not the nature of men of Ralegh's
type to give way to the settled despondency which is the
resort of less virile minds. He had still some measure
of bodily health, and his powers of intellect were as
vigorous as ever. So we find him even in the chaos of his
destiny taking stone walls for his heritage, and gaining
some surcease of his troubles.

Rumours of contemporary events penetrated to his
retreat, and we can imagine with what feelings he heard
of the struggle between the King and the Commons, the
wars in Ireland, the bungling attempts towards American
colonization, and at a later date the negotiations for
a Spanish alliance. All were matters in which his dearest
hopes were involved, and to one of his tireless energy
inaction in such times would be doubly bitter. Indeed
external events had some slight bearing on his own life, for
a preposterous suspicion of share in the Gunpowder Plot
rested upon him for some time; and the intimacy which
he formed with the young Prince Henry brought him hope
of release and a keen sorrow when death cut short the
prince's blameless life. But on the whole his hand was

---

[1] *Domestic Correspondence: James I*, vol. xix. § 112.

stayed, and he sat in his room and heard of the course of events with an interest embittered by his utter impotence to play any part.

His first intellectual interest was chemistry, which had all the fascination of an occult mystery newly bound with the bonds of an exact science. In Sir George Harvey's garden he set up a laboratory, and betook himself to experiments. But the place was an open one, and the jealous governor thought fit to make complaints of its publicity, with the result that the chemical experiments ceased, and Ralegh began gradually to find all his occupation in the practice of letters. During his imprisonment he produced the greater part of what is now printed as his work; and his activity showed itself in the writing of pamphlets of contemporary interest as well as in the preparation of his voluminous *History of the World*. The pamphlets resemble the papers which Bacon composed in his early days, his letter to the Queen on the Roman Catholic interest and his essay on *Controversies in the Church*. Such tracts were the magazine articles of the period, and influenced and reflected public opinion. Of Ralegh's productions the two most important, judged by their contemporary interest, are the *Discourses on the Savoyan Matches*. They were written at the direct request of Prince Henry; and though the proposal of which they treat ended fruitlessly, they are none the less valuable as furnishing the fullest exposition we have of Ralegh's ideas on foreign policy and international relations. His talent for historical summaries nowhere shows so clearly, and his arguments, if tinged with his excessive dislike of Spain and blindness to any possibility of co-operation, are yet on the whole cogent and reasonable. Briefly, they are these: that a Savoyan alliance would mean an alliance with a dependent country, a prince of alien religion, a weak and comparatively unimportant kingdom, and above all a kingdom so situated by nature that it could give little aid to England in peace or war. In addition, he argues the old question of the Dutch independence, and concludes with a warm advocacy of the claims of the Palatine. His Spanish hostility may partly be attributed to his imprisonment and consequent ignorance of the trend of affairs. He brought into Jacobean times ideas and catchwords which had died with Elizabeth. However we may deplore the relations of England with Spain during these years, we cannot shut our eyes to the fact that the idea of an alliance was in itself perfectly reasonable, and with the altered state of national feeling calculated to produce many advantages.

Ralegh's knowledge of naval affairs gave rise to a *Discourse on the Invention of Ships* and *Observations concerning the Royal Navy*, both in all likelihood fragments of a larger *Treatise on Naval Warfare* which the author did not live to complete. *A Breviary of the History of England under William the First* followed, a work in which he seems to have had the help of Samuel Daniel. It is impossible at this hour of day to be more than remotely interested in these tractates. They read like the hack-work of a man of vigorous and cultivated mind, and are more interesting for the light which they cast upon the author's feelings and opinions at the time than for any extraordinary insight or learning.

But the *magnum opus* of these weary prison days, the work on which Ralegh's claim to a position in literature depends, was the *History of the World*. The fact that he should have entertained such a project is a singular commentary on the ambitious, comprehensive nature of the man. It was the age of far-reaching designs, when men, fired with the wide vistas which the new philosophy opened to them, desired to 'take all knowledge for their province.' It was an eminently uncritical age, since curiously enough the dawnings of the scientific spirit are usually found in conjunction with thoroughly unscientific methods. Learning was still a vast aggregate of facts, which were repeated with painstaking diligence from book to book. It was an age when extent of knowledge, combined with imposing generalizations, chiefly won the admiration of men. In some such spirit Ralegh conceived his plan and embarked upon his task. He was heavily handicapped, for besides paucity of books, he had scarcely the linguistic attainments to enable him to compass the earlier part of his work successfully. But he had one notable endowment—an honest desire to write the truth and a mind untinged by the parasitic respect for traditions ecclesiastical and political which hampered so many of his contemporaries. Nor had he that equal vice, which later historians have not been free from, that adulation of the populace, that respect for democracy and the idols of the market-place, which turns sober history into shrieking rhetoric.

Of the matter of the History we can only say that it shows much unsifted knowledge, and a certain grandness of conception which raises it above its class. The scholar will find little of importance in the rabbinical learning and superficial classical acquirements. It is the incidental passages which redeem it, when the author leaves his narrative to draw some analogy of contemporary interest or moralize on the frailties of human life. But even here we are on the verge of error, for nothing can be more delusive than the ordinary popular conception that it is one long piece of exalted and stately English. That such passages exist every lover of good English prose knows well, but the ordinary level of writing is pedestrian and dull, and little better than much obscure contemporary work. Yet all dullness and pettiness is forgotten when we turn a page and come to some such passage as the famous one in the sixth chapter of the fifth book, where he turns aside for one moment, and from the plenitude of experience and sorrow

lays bare in noble words the triviality of man's life and the
pathos of its close.

Two qualities of the man stand out clear on the face of
his work—his laborious and persistent carefulness, and the
great heart which he bore through his misfortunes. That
a man in the later days of a busy life, in the midst of ill-
health and many griefs, and with no hope of reward, should
set about such a task as this with tireless industry may well
surprise us, and that he should show throughout a large
and kindly magnanimity may well shame us of idleness and
complaint.

But through all his labours Ralegh clung to the faint
hope of some future release. Once and again he was on
the eve of freedom, and always the cup was dashed from
his lips. The death of Prince Henry cut short his
expectations in one quarter, and the death of Salisbury in
another; but he turned elsewhere, and in his letters to
Queen Anne, Lord Carew, Lord Haddington, and the
Secretary Winwood, he strove to awake interest in a scheme
which would mean liberty and possible honour for himself
and aggrandizement to the country. He had never forgotten Guiana, and in the long leisure of these years the
story which Keymis had brought back with him from his
second voyage was often before him. The gold-mine among
the hills so grew upon his imagination that he believed that
if he could but win James' consent to an expedition thither
he might yet retrieve his credit and his fortunes. 'My Lord,'
he wrote to Haddington, 'leaving the success to God's
providence, it is a journey of honour and enterprise I offer
you, a venture feasible and certain[1].' His health broke
down under an attack of apoplexy, brought on by his new
labours. But still he kept to his scheme, and wrote to the
Lords of the Council, offering to fit out two ships at his own

---

[1] Hatfield MSS. 6177, fol. 241 (British Museum), printed in
Edwards' *Ralegh*, vol. ii. p. 393.

expense, to entrust the expedition to Keymis, and to remain
himself as hostage in the Tower.   The King refused from
his habitual caution and dislike of possible war.   But when
Villiers succeeded Somerset in the royal favour, a new
opportunity was created.   To two of the favourite's brothers
Ralegh gave £750 each, and the voice of Villiers was
enlisted in his favour.   Secretary Winwood himself was
a bitter hater of Spain, and any appeal of Ralegh's fell on
friendly ears.   The combined forces of Winwood and
Villiers worked the desired effect, and the Queen lent her
aid.   On March 19, a minute of the Privy Council declared
that ' His Majesty, out of his gracious inclination, had been
pleased to release Sir Walter Ralegh to go abroad with
a Keeper to make provision for his intended voyage [1].'

XII.

To see what Ralegh's release and projected expedition
signified in the history of the time it is necessary to go
back a little to the beginning of the English and Spanish
negotiations.   Philip III of Spain and Lerma, his minister,
had the same end in view which guided the policy of their
predecessor, but a greater prudence inspired their methods.
The hand of the Infanta, with the possibility of the matri-
monial crown of the great Spanish empire, was a coveted
prize among the sovereigns of Europe.   A marriage with
the son of the King of England had long been talked of,
which would bring the two countries into harmonious
relations and in time further the cause of Catholicism,
which the Spanish monarch had made his own.   James'
own view on the matter was at all times practically the
same.   He wished to see the nations of Europe dwelling in
unity ; nothing was more abhorrent to him than the

[1] Edwards' *Ralegh*, vol. i. p. 563; Gardiner, *Prince Chas. and
Span. Mar.* i. p. 48.

buccaneering and swashbuckling spirit which had taken captive Elizabethan minds and had crept even into the counsels of Elizabethan statesmen. Further, he felt the rottenness of the ground beneath his feet in his dealings with the Parliament and his whole attitude to the people which he governed. He could only be well disposed to an alliance with Spain if it furthered his designs of peace, refilled his exchequer, and provided him with a strong external aid in the case of domestic difficulties.

Any such natural predilections in the King's mind were jealously fostered by Diego Sarmiento de Acuña, afterwards Count of Gondomar, a diplomatist of singular tact and a man of the most resolute character. In all the bickerings with the Commons he adroitly suggested to the King the need of a strong supporting power, and by alternate use of threats and persuasion he achieved his end.

At the precise moment of Ralegh's liberation the influence of Sarmiento was counteracted by others. It is true that the marriage was practically arranged and on the eve of being publicly proclaimed, but there was a strong faction in the country, to which Villiers lent his great authority, which was vehemently opposed to the Spanish negotiations. With such men Ralegh's proposal found a ready welcome. Of James' own view of the matter it is impossible to speak with certainty. He felt that the Spanish match was necessary in the position in which he found himself, but none the less he dared not risk the opprobrium which would follow a strenuous advocacy of Spanish claims. Further, he did not admit the right of Spain to the whole of the Americas, and he regarded Guiana, in such parts as were not yet occupied by Spanish settlements, as the right of the first comer. It was true that Sarmiento had bitterly remonstrated and striven to counteract the permission given, but a large part of the Court declared that no war with Spain would follow

Ralegh's attempt, but that by his successful return the King's empty coffers might be filled and the nation appeased. It is vain to look to James for any high considerations or clear-sighted political wisdom. He might well have remembered that all previous quests for treasure had been futile, and that it was in the highest degree impolitic to scatter the national energies on two continents, when in Virginia was an English settlement which needed all the care and help which the home country could afford. But James was incapable of such reflections; he found himself between two stools, anxious to bring the Spanish match to a successful issue and fearful of offending the strong anti-Spanish faction in the country. To authorize Ralegh's expedition would temporarily satisfy them; and if the unhappy man failed there remained for him summary punishment. So on August 26 he issued a commission giving him power to search for gold in any territory not already occupied by a Christian monarch. Ralegh had previously pledged his word that the mine which he sought was not in Spanish territory; if anything miscarried the fault was his and he should bear the blame.

Few men have ever found themselves in a position more fraught with difficulties than was Ralegh's at this moment. He had staked all on Keymis' word of a gold-mine in the hills, which by this time might be exhausted or already in Spanish hands. It is important to notice a fact[1], which Mr. Gardiner seems to have abundantly proved, that the mine which Ralegh had for his goal was not, as far as he knew, in close proximity to any Spanish settlement; and consequently there is no reason to believe that he perjured himself in his declaration to the King. But he was hampered on all sides with galling restrictions. He knew something of the country, and he must have known that to penetrate far without a conflict with Spanish troops

[1] *Prince Chas. and Span. Mar.*, vol. i. pp. 53 and 54 note.

bordered on the impossible. He knew that the slightest breach of his orders would be construed on his return into a crime, and that nothing short of the most brilliant success would ensure his safety. His crews were untrustworthy, for the weight of royal disapproval lay upon him, and his old sailors did not rally round him. He embarked on his enterprise under the cloak of a deliberate falsehood, for we know of his avowed intention to justify his course by the capture of the plate fleet, if all else failed. But we can well pardon him, for to one who had lain long between four walls the thought of being once more on the open sea and among men was sufficient to make the most chimerical scheme seem fair and reasonable.

We can well understand, too, how, situated as he was, he should have let other alternative schemes occupy his mind, to which he might turn in the event of failure. A chance arose of making a breach with Spain by aiding the Duke of Savoy in his struggle with the greater monarchy. Ralegh proposed the seizure of Genoa by English troops, which would cripple the Spanish resources and bring funds to the needy king. He sent word to Scarnafissi asking him to obtain James' consent to the scheme, and for some little while it seemed as if success were possible. But James' continued distrust of Ralegh, his reluctance to engage in the inevitable Spanish war, and the tidings that the difficulties between the Duke and Spain were likely to be settled by arbitration, broke off the negotiations and threw Ralegh once more upon his old designs. But he had other strings to his bow, and he was urged by foolish friends to plans which were not only impolitic but in gross violation of his plighted word. He had always been in communication with the Huguenots, and there were not wanting those who urged him to sail for the coast of France and join his forces in the opposition to the Queen Mother. He told Desmarets, the French ambassador, that he had intentions of leaving his own country and offering his services to the King of France [1], and on the eve of his departure he sent a letter to Montmorency by a Frenchman called Faige, asking him to obtain permission for his taking refuge under certain contingencies in a French port [2]. The same emissary and another Frenchman Belle were commissioned to follow him to the Indies with four French ships which were being prepared at Havre and Dieppe. They subsequently betrayed their trust and informed the Spanish Government that Ralegh intended to use the French vessels in an attack upon San Thome, that then he was to attack Trinidad and Margarita, and finally return to Europe. It is possible that in the crisis of his affairs such plans were part of his scheme, and that he allowed his integrity to be overcome by his old desire of crippling Spain in the west and earning the King's pardon for any outrage by a lavish treasure.

Before the fleet actually set sail Sarmiento made one more strenuous effort to obtain his recall. A meeting of the Council was called to consider the matter, but Ralegh's friends outweighed the Spanish faction and he was allowed to depart in peace. Doubts of his honour seem to have troubled even his best friends. Ere he left the Thames Arundel asked him to pledge his word that he would return to England whatever befell. It shows how far the man had gone in his desperation that, although at the very moment he was intriguing with France, he unhesitatingly gave the desired promise.

The details of the voyage are dreary reading. His men were mutinous and raw, the weather was always against them, and disease made ravages in their number. Everything evil seemed fated to befall the unhappy squadron. They encountered difficulties at the Canaries. Ralegh him-

[1] Edwards' *Ralegh*, i. 595 note.
[2] Gardiner, *Prin. Charles*, p. 63 note.

self fell sick, and for ten days lay tossing with fever. The
one thing which cheered him was the discovery that his
name and deeds were not forgotten among the Indians,
and that they were willing to help any Englishman for his
sake.

As soon as he could leave his bed he anchored opposite
the Isles de Salut to consider his steps. He had ten vessels
left, but five only were serviceable for river navigation.
Extreme ill-health and the wishes of his men compelled
him to wait at the river mouth; but he prepared a force of
four hundred, over whom he put Keymis in command.
The choice was one of necessity; the servant had proved
himself gallant and trustworthy, but it remained to be seen
whether he had any of the higher qualifications of a leader.
It is clear that through all this the chance of an engagement with the Spaniards was ever present in Ralegh's mind.
Indeed, we find him actually contemplating the assault of
San Thome, and replying to the objections of his officers
by the extraordinary statement[1], 'I have order by word of
mouth of King and Council to take the town if it is any
hindrance to the digging of the mine.' We can understand
his frame of mind; worn by sickness and despair, all the
minor moralities of life sank out of his consideration, and
the end of his vision seemed limited to a courageous
death.

He sent off the band of pioneers with words which ring
like the last bravado of a doomed man. 'You shall find
me on your return at Punto Gallo, dead or alive; and if
you find not my ships there at least you shall find their
ashes. For I will fire with the galleons if it comes to
extremity; but run away I will never[2].' How much the
success of the expedition meant to him we can guess, for it
contained his son Walter as a leader of a company, and on

[1] Bacon's *Declaration* and Ralegh's *Address to Lord Carew*.
[2] Ralegh to Keymis. Cayley, *Life of Ralegh*, ii. 125.

its issue hinged his hope of life. So he set himself to wait
patiently, while a raw and ill-led band sought to achieve the
impossible.

The history of Keymis' expedition is one long record of
disaster. After three difficult weeks, in which two vessels
were left stranded behind, the three English ships came in
sight of the new settlement of San Tomàs. The sight, so
utterly unlooked for, filled them with dismay. Keymis
seems to have lost his wits, and instead of passing the town
and making an effort to reach the mine, he resolved to
attack it, in defiance of what he knew to have been the
wishes of his commander. That evening the attempt took
place. The Spaniards were found prepared, but after some
desperate fighting the English set fire to the houses and
drove out the defenders. In the melée Walter Ralegh, the
general's son, fell fighting bravely.

For some days the invaders kept their position, while the
chances of ever reaching the mine grew smaller and smaller.
The Spaniards blocked all the approaches, while the men
themselves lost heart and bitterly reproached their leader.
Keymis soon lost all hope, and even if it had still been
possible to reach the mine it is doubtful if he could have
persuaded his band to follow him. He gave up all thought
of success, and with a hopeless heart led his shattered
forces back to Ralegh in the Gulf of Paria.

The sad news had already been brought there by a wan-
dering Indian, and Keymis' letter confirmed it. Keymis
himself on his arrival did not mend matters, for he pleaded
as his excuse that the gold would have done Ralegh no
good even if he had secured it. In anger at his lieutenant's
stupidity and heart-broken at his son's death, Ralegh lost all
his self-command, and upbraided him in bitter words which
were cruel to one of Keymis' services. It was the last drop
in the cup of the unhappy man's humiliation. He saw the
full mischief he had wrought, he saw his beloved master's

affections estranged for ever; and in his desolation he sought his cabin and drove a knife into his heart.

His lieutenant's suicide was the final destruction of Ralegh's hopes. Nothing remained but a blank wall of despair, and he had recourse to desperate expedients. He tried to persuade his men to follow him to a fresh attack on the mine, in which he might succeed or fall gloriously; but the proposal met deaf ears. Then his thoughts turned to the Mexican plate-ship, and he entreated his captains to follow him in an attack upon it. If such were successful, all might yet be well[1]. His French commission, which empowered him to take anything beyond the Canaries, might satisfy the King. But his men knew the futility of such reasoning, and gave no welcome to the project. Then the unhappy fleet drifted slowly homewards, to the tribunal which should judge its captain's deeds. In this, the blackest hour of Ralegh's fate, it is to his honour that the idea of suicide, present to him on a former occasion, seems never to have entered his mind. His son was buried in the Guiana woods, a hostile court and king awaited him, and a trial of which there could be only one result. But in this stormy twilight of his life a serener dignity seemed to be with him, and he set his face to his doom with a settled and heroic resolution. We hear of him at St. Christopher with only four ships and deserted by two of his most trusted captains. Again, he is at Newfoundland, and then we hear of a mutiny in the open seas and Ralegh persuading his men with difficulty to steer for Plymouth. At length, in the beginning of June, the *Destiny* entered the English port.

Meanwhile in England all things were ready for his reception. The news of the hostilities in Guiana had given Gondomar the opportunity he desired. He went at once to James and reminded him of his promise, the conditions on which Ralegh had sailed, and the course to be taken if

---

[1] Sir T. Wilson's Report. Gardiner, iii. p. 131 note.

friendship with Spain were to be maintained. The Spanish match was still dear to James' heart. He assured the ambassador that justice would be done, that if the charge were proved Ralegh would be delivered up to the King of Spain for such punishment as he willed. On June 11 a proclamation was issued, inviting all who had evidence against the accused to come before the Council; and the Lord High Admiral ordered the seizure of the *Destiny* as soon as she appeared in English seas.

When Ralegh arrived at Plymouth and was in the act of setting out for London, he was met by his cousin, Sir Lewis Stukely, the Vice-Admiral of Devon. By him he was detained at Plymouth, but only under the loosest restraint. The idea of escape grew on his mind, and he commissioned a Captain King to find him a vessel. But Ralegh could not bring himself to a step by which he should leave the land dishonoured and obscure, and soon he was removed to London. On the road his fear got the better of him, and he feigned illness to delay the journey. When he reached the city the thought of escape returned, and he besought King to get him a ship at Gravesend.

Meanwhile a system of espionage was practised incessantly upon the prisoner by Stukely and a French physician Mannourie, in the hope of finding particulars of his suspected plot with France. Le Clerc, the King of France's agent, had sent a message by an interpreter, La Chesnée, offering him his assistance in his escape across the Channel. On his arrival he was lodged in his house in Bread Street, and thither Le Clerc came and repeated the offers. Stukely, feigning willingness to aid him, accompanied him the next morning to a boat, which he had already arranged should be stopped at Woolwich. There accordingly Ralegh was arrested and conveyed to the Tower. So closed his brief space of freedom, and now there remained only the *dénouement* of the whole tragi-comedy.

XIII.

On the eve of his imprisonment, in the days of his counterfeited sickness, Ralegh had drawn up a statement which was to be at once his report and his defence. The *Apologie for the Voyage to Guiana* may fairly rank among the best of his works. All his old tenets are defended, and his distrust of Spain is expounded in words so noble and strong as to give a fair colour even to the hazardous transactions wrought in its name. It was the full statement of a life-long policy, and we at a later day, with some knowledge of the innate greatness of the man, accept it as the final criticism on his life. But at the same time few things could be more damaging to his cause. He confessed that he had broken the terms on which he sailed, and his defiance of Spain could not be grateful to those who sought an alliance. It was with this clear admission of guilt that Ralegh entered upon his trial.

The Commission appointed to inquire into the charges against him were sadly nonplussed by the extraordinary mass of contradictions, and Ralegh's conflicting testimony did not reassure them. With natural exasperation they came to the conclusion that he was guilty in the fullest sense, and that he had deliberately deceived the King and Council by talk of a mine which did not exist and which he had no intention of seeking. On August 17 he was brought before them and confronted with the full charge. With the skill of one who had already had some experience of capital trials, he centred his defence on the weakest part of the accusation, and showed the honesty of his intentions. But he was driven to confess that he had proposed to seize the Mexican fleet, and it was hardly likely that men, already versed in his duplicity, would give him credit for sincerity, which at the best was only possible.

There was still another class of charges—those of complicity in a French plot—which a suspicious Government
urged against him.   After long equivocations he was compelled to own that he had set out with a French commission,
that the French ambassador had offered to assist him in his
escape, and that he had at various times entertained thoughts
of a refuge in France.   All this was trivial enough in itself,
but it acquires significance from the circumstances of the
time.   The relation to France was the most difficult problem
of statesmanship, and a man who was found in negotiations
with a French Government, who was a notorious liar convicted by his own words, might well be supposed to have
entered into further treasonable matters.   This hint of
a French connexion played no small part in influencing
the minds of the judges.

At length the commissioners, under Bacon's guidance,
drew up and presented their report.   The offences which
he had committed, they said, were more than sufficient to
warrant his death; but as he had never been pardoned,
he was still an attainted man, and as such could be executed
only on the old charge.   But it was necessary that the
people should know this clearly, and so they proposed two
alternatives.   A complete statement of his offences might
be published, that all might know that his death was
attributed to his former charge only by a legal formality.
Or, better still, let a public trial take place.   Let the
prisoner appear before the Council and a select body of
judges, the house being thrown open to certain peers and
private gentlemen, who would act as public witnesses of the
transaction.   The second alternative James could not
entertain.   He had no desire to hear the tissue of absurdities
which he called his policy denounced with the unsparing
force of one who was beyond any earthly fear.   It was
possible even that the Spanish proposals might suffer in
consequence.   So he contented himself with directing the

judges of the King's Bench to give judgement on the old sentence.

On October 28 Ralegh was brought before the bar to hear his doom. He was told by Yelverton that he was to be condemned on the previous Winchester verdict, unless he could show a clear pardon from the King. Ralegh in vain brought forward the plea that his commission stood in lieu of a pardon, and finding this of no avail, declared that he threw himself upon the King's mercy. Accordingly Montague pronounced the sentence of death.

In all this the thread of motive is perfectly clear. James had brought himself into a position which demanded either Ralegh's sacrifice or his own humiliation. He had been largely responsible for the ill-fated expedition, but he chose not to recognize an obligation which depended only upon honour. It is clear, too, that Ralegh had erred grossly both in judgement and conduct. We may pardon his readiness to engage in an all but hopeless errand when we think of his nature and his long captivity, but we cannot wonder that he had to bear the consequences. We can find, too, abundant excuse for the graver fault of his broken promise and deliberate falsehood, but we do not wonder that he had to pay the penalty. The peculiar hardship of his position lay in the fact that he was condemned with doubtful law and more than doubtful justice. An expedition had been undertaken with certain expectation of failure, but yet with the connivance of the King. On this expedition he had been guilty of faults worthy of death, but it is almost certain that if he had been tried on this question he would have been condemned illegally. His judges would have centred their indictment on their assumption of his consistent falsehood, and not only would they have failed to substantiate it, but a strong chain of counter-evidence could have been produced. Again, it is possible that if this had been his only crime James would have risked a breach with Spain rather than admit of a trial which would inevitably have shown himself and his designs in an odious light. As it was, the real point of his offence was concealed under a legal quibble. Here, too, there was a rankling injustice, for most judges would admit the force of Ralegh's plea that the King's commission represented a pardon. Yet, apart from the tortuous unfairness of the methods employed, we are compelled to admit that his condemnation was broadly a just one. He had broken the law of the realm in more ways than one—with abundant cause it is true, and in an heroic fashion, but still with criminal purpose. The ends of common justice could only be satisfied with his death.

Throughout these last days his conduct was at first querulous and uncertain. He upbraided his best friends, accused Winwood of betrayal of confidence, and suffered his sorrows to cloud the natural kindliness of his temper. The life of intrigue and falsehood which he had lately lived had not been without its effect. But the near approach of death seemed to raise him to a lofty and settled calm. Indeed, the death of Ralegh, with its note of rhetoric and its clear sound of genuine heroism, is a singular commentary on his eager, turbid life. With the bravado which had always been a feature of his character, he used his last speech as both an apology and a defence. Every step of his progress to the scaffold has been made the centre of a tale, which was told to succeeding generations of Englishmen who had forgotten the great captain's faults in his achievements. Ere he turned to the executioner he closed his declaration with a brief prayer for pardon. 'I have been a man full of vanity, who has lived a sinful life in such callings as have been most inducing to it; for I have been a soldier, a sailor, and a courtier, which are courses of wickedness and vice. I pray that His Almighty Goodness will forgive me; that He will cast away my sins from me, and that He will raise me into everlasting life.' With such words we 'shut up the story of his days.'

XIV.

The immediate result of his death was that his name became at once foremost in men's thoughts and affections. His great national services, the zeal with which he had urged war against the national enemy, the last pathetic scenes of his life, were all remembered, and the causes of his former unpopularity were forgotten. It was with something like vengeful satisfaction that the nation witnessed the luckless fate of Ralegh's enemies—Stukely, Mannourie, and Cobham. So strong was the national feeling that Bacon, under the direction of the Court of Commissioners, proceeded to prepare his statement of the reasons which led to Ralegh's death. Eulogists have lavished much undeserved abuse upon this production, but it is hard to regard it with complete equanimity. Reasonable and fair though it is in many parts, it has the central fault that it assumes Ralegh's intended fraud from the beginning, and, proceeding upon this assumption, distorts facts and discolours motives.

Nor did this popularity wane during the succeeding generations. The new school of politicians who were to fight the battle of constitutional freedom found in Ralegh a precursor and an exemplar. 'All history,' wrote Eliot, who witnessed the execution, 'scarcely contains a parallel to the fortitude of *our* Ralegh,' and a sense of intellectual kinship endeared his name to Pym, Hampden, Cromwell, and Milton. In him they saw a martyr to the cause of liberty, one done to death by a tyrant king. Yet it cannot be too strongly emphasized that Ralegh's death had scarcely any political significance. He fell in consequence of his own errors, through the treachery of enemies, but certainly through no arbitrary decision of a king. His importance lay not in his championship of a political cause, but in the influence which a life so brilliant, and at its best so worthy, exercised upon the national mind.

After the reputation which accrued to him as a supposed friend of liberty or as the uncompromising foe of Spain had died away, there remained the attraction of a singularly gifted personality and the glamour of a bold career. When we have weighed his work in the balances, and found its final value to be this or that, little or great as it may be, there still remains the figure of a great man. His fame is infinitely greater than the exact place which he fills in history. Through all the imperfections and failures of his life there shines out a soul, rich and essentially of noble quality. To us he is still the type of the living and heroic spirit which filled a great epoch of time.

And it is this, this spiritual quality, which makes any estimate of the man according to the success which he obtained in his various activities radically unfair. The popular verdict is still the truer. We call him a great scholar, humanist, and man of letters, but what proofs has he left us? His *History* is full of noble things, but invertebrate, inadequate, and uncritical. Few of the poems which go by his name can be proved conclusively to be his, and even these are little above the level of a minor lyricist. He is ranked with Bacon as one of the leaders of the new learning, and all he has left us consist of two metaphysical treatises, *The Sceptic* and the *Treatise on the Soul*, which are peculiarly barren and conventional. He is believed to be one of our great commanders by land and sea, and on what grounds? A few minor successes in desultory Irish wars, the report of good advice given to Essex at Cadiz, a few secondary positions competently filled, and a great and signal failure on the one occasion on which he was wholly unfettered. He is the founder of English colonies, but his particular attempts in Guiana ended disastrously, and it was many years after his death before the Virginian settlement was fully established.

The same difficulty—this contrast between hard fact and popular reputation—meets us in any consideration of his character. If not like Sir Philip Sidney, a 'model of harmonious gentleman,' he is at least to most men a type of strenuous, high-souled, and single-eyed patriotism, of all the more heart-stirring virtues. But history shows him mean and all but treacherous on many occasions, unscrupulous in ambition, many times cruel and self-seeking. And even in the minor qualities our estimate must waver. He loved his wife, but he began by wronging her; he was a good master to his servants, but at times he could show hardness and injustice. His devoutness has been made the subject of eloquent eulogy, but there seems abundant proof that in his own day his piety was regarded as doubtful at the best[1]. His character has always been supposed to rest upon his sterling honesty of purpose, and yet we find him on more occasions than one in palpable falsehood.

Yet all this damning evidence does not substantially alter the truth of the popular judgement. He was great in gifts and great in character. That resolute desire which can alone raise a man to the highest place was never his, and consequently, in spite of a hundred talents and an indomitable will, he fell short of actual attainment. If he had curbed his aims and centred his interests on almost any human activity, on literature, statesmanship, warfare,

---

[1] He was accused in company with Marlowe and others of being a member of an atheistical society. Archbishop Abbot attributed his death to his questioning 'God's being and omnipotence.' (Abbot to Roe, Feb. 19, 1618–19.) But this report had probably its only foundation in the active inquiring character of his mind. On one occasion he is said to have sat up all night talking on religious topics with the Jesuit John Comatius (Foley's *Jesuits*, iii. 461–462). We have also Harrington's testimony (*Nugae Antiquae*, ii. 132) that 'in religion he hath shown in private talk great depth and good reading.'

colonizing, on the mere life of the Court, his influence would sooner or later have become dominant. But the multiplicity of his interests, while it renders him an infinitely brilliant and romantic figure, hindered him from tangible achievement.

This over-wide mental activity finds its counterpart, if not its source, in his defects of character. To such we must attribute his greater misfortunes. The broad qualities of honour and charity were always present, but he lacked that nice scrupulousness which carries them into all the details of life. His unpopularity and his hardships were more directly consequent upon his frequent pride and asperity of manner, his more frequent lack of pride in undertaking unworthy business, his use of ignoble means, and his ill-judged temper, than upon the tricks of fate or a malignant king. He failed of success and he fell upon trouble from the same lack of consistent purpose.

But his great worth, his dazzling career, and his natural faults serve only to make him more attractive, more human. For his life is great tragedy in the fullest sense, a profound and moving presentment of the nature of man. In a singular degree he realizes the Greek conception of the ideal tragic hero, a man of like qualities with our own, yet transcending them in a certain nobleness, who suffers not through deliberate wrong-doing, but from a flaw in character, a certain fatal error in conduct, and whose very virtues, in the irony of life, serve to hasten his fate. And after the consideration of his career we come back to the popular verdict to acknowledge its truth, and see in this great Englishman one who loved his country well and fought in difficult days a good fight for her well-being,— above all a man, who through frequent stumbling lived his life bravely and fully, and bequeathed to his countrymen the legacy of a great example.

www.ingramcontent.com/pod-product-compliance
Lightning Source LLC
Chambersburg PA
CBHW030007030726
47499CB00008B/2931